THE RAIN BARREL BABY

THE RAIN BARREL BABY

ALISON PRESTON

Signature
EDITIONS

Cover photo by Paul Martens.
Cover design by Terry Gallagher/Doowah Design.
Printed and bound in Canada by AGMV Marquis Imprimeur.

Thanks to The Canada Council for the Arts and the Manitoba Arts Council for financial support during the writing of this book.

Also, thanks to Catherine Hunter, Sharon Riches, Rand Steeves, Wayne Tefs, and Chris Thompson. Special thanks to Bruce Gillespie and Karen Haughian.

We acknowledge the support of The Canada Council for the Arts and the Manitoba Arts Council for our publishing program.

Canadian Cataloguing in Publication Data

Preston, Alison, 1949–
        The rain barrel baby

ISBN 0-921833-73-3

        I. Title.

PS8581.R44R35 2000   C813'.54   C00-901207-9
PR9199.3.P74R44 2000

Signature Editions, P.O. Box 206, RPO Corydon
Winnipeg, Manitoba, R3M 3S7

for John

CHAPTER 1
1954

"A boy drowned here last year."

The words drift over on the wind to the family of three sitting on the beach at Matlock. They don't know where the words come from. Sounds on the beach are tricky. You can hear a laugh or a bark from a mile away. But sometimes the words of the person lying next to you get lost in the waves.

The mother slathers cocoa butter on herself and tells the boy to do the same. When he's done, he smoothes some onto the back of the little girl.

"Don't waste it, Ray," the mother says. "There's not very much left in the jar. Your sister doesn't really need it."

"Yes she does." He keeps on till she is well covered. "There's still lots left."

Ray is seven and he wears two hats. One is a black cap with the name Gophers embroidered in gold thread. Gophers is the name of his pee-wee ball team. Ray plays first base. He chose the cap when the mother told him to be sure to bring a hat. He didn't know she was talking about sun protection. She has placed one of her big straw hats on top of it. He doesn't seem to mind.

Squinting into the sun, the girl smiles up at her brother. He smiles back and removes his hats to go for a swim.

"Be careful out there!" the mother shouts as Ray dives into the waves. "A little boy drowned here last year, ya know."

Her words vanish before they reach Ray's ears but the girl hears them and shivers.

"Time for some sand cakes," the mother says, and helps her daughter cut out tiny squares from the damp sand near the shore.

"Mmm," the mother says and pretends to eat one. "You now. Take a bite."

The girl sits in the wet sand with the water lapping around her. She is three, going on four.

"I don't want to, Mummy. I don't want to eat sand."

"You know you have to, so just do it," the mother says and smiles up at the people walking by. "And don't forget to chew."

It scrapes against her tiny teeth, grinds in her ears. It's louder than the waves. She gags on sand and tears, feels as though her head is made of sand and she could just lie down and be part of the shoreline.

"Clean yourself up now, before your brother sees you all grubby and dirty."

The little girl leans over the shallows and splashes water onto her face. She peers into the lake, hoping to see a fish or some smooth stones at the bottom, hoping to see anything. But the lake is cloudy and dark. And the darkness settles inside her narrow chest.

CHAPTER 2
The Present

"Greta Bower found a baby in her rain barrel," Gus said.

Frank Foote turned cold. He stepped out onto his front porch and closed the door behind him. "What?"

"Well, I guess, technically, I found it," Gus said. "She asked me if I could come over and give her a hand with her rain barrel." He gave his head a shake. "It was awful."

"Is it...alive?"

"No, Frank. It's dead. Real dead."

"Oh, God." Frank clutched his thinning hair in both fists. "Whose baby is it?" he asked. "Where did it come from?"

"I don't know. It hardly looks like a baby anymore. It's been in the barrel quite a while I guess." Gus sat down on the top step. "I think maybe it wintered there."

"I'm sorry, Gus. Let me get you a glass of water. You're as white as a sheet."

"No sheet of mine, that's for sure. Since Irma died mine just keep gettin' grayer and grayer."

Frank returned with the water. "So Greta doesn't have any ideas on it?"

"She doesn't seem to. She just started to shake and hasn't stopped."

"Where is she?" Frank asked.

"I took her to my place." Gus took a sip of water and spit it out. "She wanted to get away from it."

"I don't blame her." Frank sat down on the step beside his friend. "Are you sure it's a baby?" he asked. "Maybe it's a raccoon or a squirrel or something. Sometimes foxes come into town."

"It's a baby all right," Gus said. "I think I can tell a human being from a fox. Jesus, Frank."

"Sorry, Gus. Just hoping I guess."

The morning was cool, too cool to be sitting on the porch in shirtsleeves the way Frank was. Chilly sweat slid down his sides and a gust of wind brought goose bumps out on his forearms. "Where is it now?" he asked.

"It's still in the bottom of the barrel. I drained it. Ya see, her water had been cloudy lately and got to smellin' kinda funny. That's why she asked me to come over and have a look at it for her. After the water was emptied out I stood on her ladder to take a peek inside."

"God, I'm sorry you had to see it, Gus. I don't expect it was a very pretty sight."

"I've seen plenty of death in my time, Frank. I grew up on a farm. But yeah, this is the worst…the worst I can remember."

Frank put his arm around the thin shoulders of his next-door neighbour, just for a moment. "Who the hell has a rain barrel around here anymore?" he asked.

"Greta Bower. That's who. She's pretty upset, Frank. I should probably get back to my place. I just kind of put her on the couch and left her."

"Yeah, you're right, Gus. We better get moving. I'm just going to have a word with Emma and then I'll come over. I don't want my kids to know about this."

"Thanks, Frank. I'll see ya in a few minutes then."

Frank brushed his teeth and spoke to Emma, who agreed to watch Garth and Sadie.

"It's Sunday," she said. "I thought this was your day off."

"Yeah, it is, but there's a little problem at Greta Bower's place. I'm just going to check it out and then I'll phone the station and get someone else out to clear it up."

"Was that Mr. Olsen at the door?" Emma asked. "What happened? Did someone die?"

"Don't worry about it, Em. I'm sure it's nothing."

Greta was a wreck. Gus had given her a mug of brandy even though it was just mid-morning.

She explained about the rain barrel. "It's just always been there. It was there when I was a kid and…well, I like it. I use the water for my plants and my hair and that's about it."

She combed her fingers through her crinkly auburn hair run through with gray. "It makes it nice and soft." She smiled at Frank, who sighed.

He had known Greta Bower since school days, her and her stepbrothers, though the brothers were both long gone. She and her mother had moved into the Simkin house when Mrs. Bower married Leo and became Mrs. Simkin.

Frank didn't know what had happened to Greta's first dad, only that she missed him enough to keep his name.

Her second dad, Leo, was a bit of a tyrant. Both brothers used to come to school with black eyes and various other bruises. He left Greta alone as far as Frank knew. At least there was never anything that showed. Leo took off when the kids were still in school, leaving the new Mrs. Simkin with three kids to support instead of one. They never saw him again; no one tried very hard to find him.

Mrs. Simkin went back to nursing, which was what she had done before she met her first husband, Mr. Bower. A lot of the load was put on Greta, the running of the house and the care of her brothers, even though they were slightly older.

Duane and Dwight Simkin responded to their lot in life by growing huge and running wild.

Greta became a homebody, hanging on to the only bit of security she'd ever known: the great rambling house on Claremont Avenue. It was paid for. Her mother had seen to that before she died.

"The water got kind of yucky looking lately," Greta said now, "and it had a bit of a stink to it, so I quit using it. I thought maybe the barrel needed cleaning or something. There's a filter on top to keep out biggish things and I did have it covered with lengths of wood over the winter, but I figured maybe lots of small insects added up, or maybe some kid did something. Oh hell, I don't know what I figured."

Greta gulped down the rest of her brandy and Gus poured her some more.

"The filter is really just resting there," she said. "Anyone could move it if they had something to stand on. Could you please make it go away Frank? I'd really like to get it cleaned up in a hurry. It's supposed to rain tonight."

"You're surely not going to use it again after this?" Gus said.

"Why not? It's just a little baby. What could be more natural than that?" She laughed. "Maybe it'll give my hair new life."

She's lost her marbles, Frank thought. Maybe it's just temporary, from the shock. Or, maybe she belongs in a loony bin.

"You're thinking I'm crazy, aren't you?" Greta said. "I can tell by the look on your face." She started to cry.

Frank felt terrible, the way he always did when women cried, as though it were his fault and it was up to him to fix things. He touched her shoulder and gave her a handkerchief.

"No, Greta. No one's thinking you're crazy. It just surprised me is all. Most people would probably want to get rid of the rain barrel after something like this. But you're right. A poor dead baby is nothing to run from."

Gus didn't look so sure. He fetched a glass and poured some brandy for himself.

Frank left the room to phone the police station.

He admired Greta in a way, with her compost heap, her lawn of wild flowers and grasses in the summer, her herb and vegetable garden, and her luscious desserts. She ran a baking business out of her house, selling her cheesecakes and profiteroles, her tortes and her fruit pies to the fine restaurants and delis of Winnipeg.

Frank always knew if he was eating something that she made. "Is this a Greta Bower?" he has asked many times when he has stepped out for a treat on his lunch hour or ordered dessert after a rare dinner out. Frank's sweet tooth was famous and it took more than doughnuts to satisfy it. The way he figured it was, if you were going to do it, do it up right. Not that doughnuts didn't have their place.

Frank made the call. There was a Patrol Sergeant just a few minutes away.

Frank had gone out with Greta a couple of times in the long ago days of high school, when he and his girlfriend Audrey had been on the outs.

But Greta had been too peculiar for him and she wasn't any less so now. She still looked like a hippie with her wild hair and flowing skirts. A lonesome middle-aged hippie with a dead baby in her rain barrel.

"Let's go over there now, the three of us," Frank said when he was off the phone. "We should be there when they arrive."

"Who?" Greta asked.

"The people who are coming to take the baby away and launch the investigation. The cops."

Frank felt as though he was talking to a four-year-old. Sadie would've had a better grasp of this and she was just six.

He looked at the two of them drinking on Gus' couch, staring at him with eyes a few degrees off the mark.

"I'm afraid your property will have to be treated as a crime scene for a little while, Greta."

"Oh dear," she moaned. "I had thought maybe we could just have a small service, the three of us, in my backyard and then bury the little tyke out there, past the vegetable garden."

Frank eyed the brandy bottle.

"I could sing a song," she added.

He took a swig right from the bottle and gagged. The taste reminded him of how sick he felt sometimes on days when everything was going well.

"Let's go, you two. I hear sirens. I don't know what the hell they hope to accomplish with all that racket."

"Do I have to go too?" Gus asked.

"I'm afraid so, Gus," Frank sighed. "It shouldn't take long."

It's way better when I don't know the people involved, Frank thought, as he herded his neighbours out onto the street where a crowd was beginning to gather. This was feeling a little too close to home.

He wondered where Greta's stepbrothers were these days. Could this baby be connected to either of them in some way? He would have to ask her about their whereabouts. He'd happily lost track of Duane and Dwight, though he'd known them both better than he'd wanted to in the old days.

He had even known who Gus was way back when. It was that kind of neighbourhood.

It was a girl baby and the medical examiner gave the order to take it away. Frank managed not to see it till it was wrapped and ready for its tiny body bag.

Greta cried again.

"I have a daughter, Frank. Did you know that? In 1968 I had a little girl. My mum made me give her away."

Gus had gone home and Frank and Greta were sitting across from each other at her huge kitchen table. It was an amazing kitchen, totally remodeled to accommodate Greta's baking business.

"No," Frank said. "No, Greta, I didn't know. I'm sorry." He looked around him. "This is some kitchen! Real professional."

"She's twenty-seven now," Greta said. "A full-fledged woman."

"Edgin' up on us," Frank said.

"Yeah. So you didn't know? It felt to me at the time like everybody knew."

"No," Frank repeated and wished he had brought Gus' brandy with him. Talking to Greta made him uncomfortable.

"I named her Jane before they took her away. They let me hold her for a while. I didn't know then if the people who took her would know she was called Jane or if they would keep it as her name, but that's what I called her. Would you like to see a picture?"

When Greta left the room Frank read the clipped cartoons attached to one of her fridges—she had two. She liked *Calvin and Hobbes*. So did Frank.

She had cut out the one where Calvin says: "My watch tells the time, the day, and the date. It doesn't tell what month it is, though. I need a watch that tells the month." And Hobbes says: "I suppose they figure if you don't know what month it is, you're not the type who'd wear a watch."

Frank was chuckling when Greta came back with a photograph in a little gold frame.

"Having fun, Frank?" She looked confused.

"Sorry." He sat back down and looked at the picture of a newborn baby with its eyes closed. It had a thatch of dark hair atop its head and Frank could see Greta in its tiny face.

"She's beautiful, Greta." Frank tried to imagine what it would have been like to hold his own newborn daughter in his arms, see himself in her small face and then hand her over to a woman in white who would never bring her back.

"I wish whoever put that little girl in the rain barrel had knocked on my door instead," Greta said, tears streaming down her face. "I would have taken the baby off her hands, no question. If only she'd known that this was a door she could have knocked on."

"Oh, Greta," Frank said. "Is there someone you can call to come and stay with you awhile?"

"No. It's okay."

A huge smoky cat leapt up onto the kitchen table.

"Hi, Ailsa." Frank had met the cat before. She roamed the neighbourhood.

Ailsa pressed her face against his. He objected to a cat on a table especially when he ate cakes and tarts prepared on it. But he said nothing.

"Atta girl." Frank scratched Ailsa's ears and she flopped down on her side, so he rubbed her stomach.

Greta had stopped crying and was snuffling quietly into Frank's handkerchief.

"Will Ailsa be company enough for you then, Greta? I really should be getting home to my kids."

"Yes. I'm feeling quite tired after all this. I'll probably lie down for a nap."

"We'll let you know if anything develops," Frank said, "but to tell you the truth I don't have a lot of hope that we'll ever get to the bottom of this." He stood up to go. "The trail's pretty darn cold."

"Thanks, Frank. Thanks for everything."

"It could be a kid's baby," Frank said, mostly to himself, and thought again of Emma and her nutcase friend, Delia. Not them, but some other kid.

"Or someone too sick or tired or crazy for a baby," he said, and thought of his wife, Denise, and Greta Bower. Not them, but some other sick or crazy woman.

"Where are your brothers these days?" Frank asked. "What are they up to?" He tried to sound casual, friendly, so she wouldn't think he suspected them of anything.

Greta was getting heavy lidded. "Stepbrothers."

"Sorry. Stepbrothers."

"Duane's in prison in Quebec. For the long haul. And Dwight's dead, has been since 1983. To tell you the truth, I'm glad he's dead. And I'm glad Duane's in jail. I hope he never gets out. It would turn my life upside down if he ever came home."

"Like a baby in a rain barrel?" said Frank.

"Worse than that."

Frank pushed his chair in flush with the table and gave Ailsa a last scratch under her chin. He wondered what had killed Dwight Bower, but wanted very badly to go home right now.

"I'll see ya, Greta."

Her eyes were closed and she didn't reply. Did she not know that her robe was gaping open and that her breasts were in full view? Maybe not. Frank sighed and slipped out the back door. Maybe not.

CHAPTER 3

"He's been in love with you for, like, ever," Delia said.

"He has not!" Emma shouted.

They were smoking cigars at the swollen river's edge and talking about Donald and Vince, the boys they thought about the most.

"Ew! What's that?" Delia asked.

"What's what?" Emma glanced over her shoulder to where Delia stared, distaste scrunching up her smooth young face.

"I think it's something dead," Delia said.

Then Emma saw the cloudy eyes and the dull matted fur. "Let's get out of here."

Delia picked up a stick and poked at the dead thing, disturbing its grave of mouldy leaves.

"Delia, don't!" Emma screamed. "For God's sake, leave it alone!"

"What's the matter with you?"

"Nothing's the matter with me." Emma started up the path to the road. "What's the matter with you, for Christ's sake, fooling around with something gross and dead?"

Delia threw her stick over the cliff into the Red River.

It was rolling towards its destination in Lake Winnipeg. The spring melt this year tested the banks all along the river's run through the city and beyond.

"It's just a little furry animal." Delia brushed dust off her falling-down jeans and followed her friend up to Lyndale Drive.

"But it's dead!" Emma's hands were on her hips, scolding. "Its fur isn't even furry anymore."

"So what! It probably lived a full and happy life."

"So why does that mean you have to poke around at it with a stick? Sometimes you gross me out completely."

"Well, thanks very much!" Delia was still smoking her cigar in full view of the cars whizzing by on the drive.

Emma sighed. "I gotta go, Dele. I'll phone ya later."

"'Kay."

"Dele?" Emma turned back to her friend.

"What?" She was blowing smoke rings above her head.

Perfect smoke rings. Emma was filled with admiration. She had never been able to manage one.

"Don't get caught with that thing. If you get grounded I won't have anyone decent to talk to."

Later, in the kitchen, Emma said to her dad, "We saw something dead down at the river."

"What kind of a something dead?" Frank's stomach turned. He thought of last Sunday and pictured the swaddled baby from the rain barrel. Then he imagined it beneath its shroud and wondered why he had to do that to himself.

"Something that was once furry but is now just dead," Emma said.

"For sure it was once furry?" Frank pictured slime, not fur. He threw the dish cloth he had been wiping the counter with down the cellar stairs.

"Yeah." Emma looked at her father as though he was asking the wrong questions.

Frank wondered if dead babies ever had a furry look to them. He supposed it was possible. He had heard of babies being born with a coat of hair that was almost always shed soon after birth. Almost always.

"Not hairy, but furry?" Frank found a fresh dish cloth in a drawer and resumed his chore.

"Yeah. Dad, what's with you? You're freakin' me out."

"Sorry, Em. It's okay to have seen a dead animal at the river. They have to go somewhere to die and I guess the river is as good a place as any. Why does it smell like cigars in here? Emma, why do you smell like cigars?"

"I don't know." Emma was spreading Friday's *Free Press* out on the kitchen table.

"Have you been smoking a cigar?"

"I don't know."

"Jeez, Emma, I hope you didn't inhale at least."

"No, Dad. And I won't likely be doing it again either."

"Well, good! Was it Delia who put you up to it?"

"No! I am capable of doing something without Delia putting me up to it, you know. Why do you always think bad things about my best friend in the whole world?"

"I don't know. Aren't her pants kinda big?" Frank rinsed his cloth and draped it over the window crank to dry.

"All the kids' pants are kinda big, Dad. Look!" Emma pulled up her sweatshirt to reveal her own jeans hanging four inches below her belly-button.

"Good God, Emma! What if they fall down?"

"They did once, actually." Emma laughed. "At a football game, when I jumped up to cheer. But I had a long shirt on, so it was okay. I mean, everybody laughed and made fun of me and everything, but it was okay. I always wear a big shirt."

"What's the point of it?" Frank asked. "The big pants, I mean."

"They're comfy."

"How can they be, if you have to worry about them falling off?"

"They are."

"Yeah, okay. Well, what about all Delia's makeup and weird hair and everything?"

"She's artistic, is all. And she's not a bad influence on me. She listens to me and has all kinds of great ideas."

"Like smoking cigars at the river?" Frank smiled.

"No! Da-ad!"

"Sorry."

There I go, apologizing, Frank thought. He had made a promise to himself to say "I'm sorry" fewer times each day than was his custom, but he never remembered till after the fact.

"Dead things scare me," Emma said.

She turned to the obituaries. First, page two, for the short version, and then Section C, with its full pages of deaths, the long versions, with photographs and whole life stories. A picture of a young girl in a baseball cap smiled up at her: Esme Jones, 1982-1995.

"Jesus," Emma said.

"Jesus?" Frank turned to face Emma from his spot at the sink.

"Yeah. This person who's dead is about my age."

"Do you ever read about anything except who died?"

"Yeah, of course. I just start with the deaths. In case somebody I know dies. I hate the thought of not knowing that someone is dead. I almost feel as though I should know without being told."

"What do you say to pizza for supper?" Frank transferred yesterday's dry dishes from the rack into the cupboards. "Garth and Sadie are both keen on it."

"Where's Mum?"

"She's havin' a bit of a lie down. She's a little under the weather."

Emma snorted. "Yeah. Pizza's fine, Dad. I don't want any meat, though."

"We'll get two, so we'll all be happy. Garth, Sadie!" He spoke as loudly as he dared in the direction of the living room. "We're having pizza!"

Quiet hooting sounds made their way back to the kitchen. No one wanted to wake Denise.

Frank watched Emma stare at the face of Esme Jones. He saw the private thoughts come and go on her lovely little face. What did she imagine about the dead girl? Did she picture her alive and loving a boy? Or dead? And the thing at the river. Was she going to dream of that as well? Frank looked over her shoulder at the photograph and wondered if his daughter pictured her own face where Esme's grinned up at her above the words: "Suddenly, on May 3."

"She died suddenly," Emma said.

Frank sighed. "Well, she probably didn't suffer then."

"She looks younger than me, don't ya think, in this picture?" Emma held it up for her dad's inspection.

"Maybe it's not a recent photograph."

"Maybe not. It says here: Longer obituary to follow."

"Well, we'll have to keep our eyes peeled for that, won't we?" Frank said. "Run and get your brother and sister now and we'll figure out this pizza business."

CHAPTER 4

At dusk, a Lincoln Town Car cruised slowly down Frank Foote's street. He wasn't around to see it but Gus Olsen was, and he didn't like the look of it. The tinted windows hid the driver. He couldn't even tell if it was a man or a woman. It could have been a bear cub for all he knew. That's how dark the glass was. He didn't like the look of it, with its slowness and its windows.

Gus trusted his instincts. He knew when something wasn't right. Like the time he had mentioned to Frank that he felt uneasy about not seeing old lady Rundle for a few days. Sure enough, they found her sitting dead in her easy chair, supper stiff on her lap and the TV blaring at her no-good ears.

He hadn't seen the rain barrel business coming though. The rain barrel business flew in out of the blue.

The car was the colour of Lake Winnipeg. What colour is that? Gus wondered. What name did the car people give to a vehicle that's the same colour as the lake? Maybe Frank would know.

The car rounded the corner and edged out of sight. Gus sat down on his front steps and imagined being at the lake. He loved it there. It had been years, but maybe he could try to get out there for a few days this summer, or at least a day. He could take the bus. The west side of the lake was his favourite. The sand wasn't quite as fine as on the east side, but he felt more at home there.

The car passed by again, this time even more slowly. It stopped outside Frank's house. Then it crept forward and stopped in front of Gus.

The window slid down halfway and he could see a woman's head behind a huge pair of sunglasses.

How can she possibly see to drive? The sun has set, the car windows are almost black and she has sunglasses on to boot.

"Excuse me, sir," she said in a voice low enough to irritate Gus. Now he was going to have to get up and go towards the car if he wanted to hear what she had to say. And he did. He moved slowly and that bothered him too. He knew that what she saw was an old man, a crippled-up old man. And that infuriated him.

A year from now he'd be moving a damn sight more sprightly. Gus was in line for a new knee and his doctor had told him it would be this summer at the latest.

"Does a Frank Foote live next door to you in that house with the five windows?" the woman asked.

What the hell kind of way was that to describe a house? Five windows!

"What's a frank foot and who's askin'?" Gus felt protective of Frank, who was the best neighbour he'd ever had. Him and poor Denise and their three kids. Even the kids were good neighbours. The youngest one, Sadie, helped him with his vegetables in the summer. She thinned his carrots and talked him into keeping even the tiniest of the potatoes. She was a bit bossy for a youngster, maybe, but in his experience most women were that way. Right from the get-go.

"Frank Foote's the name of a man, sir, and I'm just an old friend." She tried to smile but it didn't work. Maybe it was all that red lipstick weighing down her lips.

Why did women always do that to themselves? he wondered. They troweled it on so you could no longer get any idea of what they really looked like. It pissed him off, the same as it pissed him off to be called sir. He didn't believe that Frank would have such a friend.

"Sorry ma'am, I wouldn't know." There. He'd called her ma'am. See how she liked that.

"And the Simkins, they live there, don't they?" she asked, pointing at Greta Bower's house. Gus looked at her again, the red lips and the smooth black hair.

"What colour would you call this car?" he asked, his fingers clutching the glass of the part-way-down window.

It started to slide up and the car moved forward.

"And how can you see to drive behind all that tinted glass?" he shouted as he was forced to let go his grip on the window.

She burned rubber as she sped away.

Gus felt a certain amount of satisfaction from his encounter. He'd have to tell Frank about the way he'd handled the strange woman. Snooping around the neighbourhood. Ha. He could hardly wait to tell Frank about how he'd run her off.

CHAPTER 5

The Norwood Flats was a town in itself, in the middle of the larger city. A triangle with river on two sides, main drag on the third. Lower middle and middle class. Some homes were almost a century old but most were built after the Second World War. Young families, young trees, lots of sunshine and Kick the Can for a couple of decades.

It was blue and gold to look back on, but Frank Foote knew better than that. Horrible things had happened in the middle of the century—he had seen some of them.

"Denise? How's it goin'?" Frank spoke into his desk phone, a familiar tightness in his throat as he talked to his wife of fifteen years.

She spoke so quietly he could hardly hear her.

"Okay, I think. It's good I'm here."

"I miss you," he lied. He covered his eyes with his hand.

"Yeah, me too. I'm sorry, Frank, I gotta go. I'm so very, very tired."

Frank hung up and took his coffee to the window. He was lucky to have one that opened. He pushed it up and took a deep breath of the cold spring air. It had been the longest, coldest, snowiest winter in decades and Frank could still feel it in his bones. He pictured himself on a beach somewhere soaking up the sun, getting so hot he felt dizzy and then wading into the water to cool down.

Frank didn't usually come to work on Sundays but he wanted to review the paperwork on the rain barrel baby. And truth be told, he wanted to get away on his own for short while. Emma was home with the kids.

Frank did miss Denise. He missed his wife of fifteen years ago when she had been smart and kind and funny. Now the sparkle in her hazel eyes was gone. She looked only inward. And when she smiled she pressed her lips together till they disappeared. She looked as though she was trying with all her might to shut out the world.

"Leave me alone!" her smile shouted.

Frank felt two ways about this new smile of hers. When she used it on him and the kids he felt bereft. When she used it on anyone else he breathed relief. He wanted her to shut out the rest of the world. And in the past when her old smile, her rich open smile had been for him and Emma and Garth and Sadie, Frank had felt blessed. But when it had shone out to others...well, he wasn't proud of those feelings. He'd rather not think about them.

She was in the Detox Ward now; she had been there before.

Yesterday, Frank had stopped by home in the mid-afternoon to check on his kids. He worried about them, especially Emma. He found her in the kitchen making sandwiches for the two younger ones.

"Hi, guy. Kinda late for lunch, isn't it?" Frank tousled her hair.

He could hear television noise from the living room where the other two would be gazing transfixed. It was probably Garth and Sadie he should be concerned about with their TV fixation. Maybe all that was foisted upon Em would make her a stronger more resourceful person, with only the odd pocket of anxiety that wouldn't get too odd.

"Hi, Dad." Emma's face lit up when she saw her father. She kept on with the bread and lettuce and sliced hard-boiled eggs. "We were pretty late with breakfast this morning."

"Where's your mum?"

"Upstairs lying down. She's been out to the mall but she didn't buy anything." Emma spread tidy amounts of mayo on one side of each sandwich and finished them off with a couple of grinds of pepper.

"How did you get along holding the fort this morning?"

"No problemo. But I think something should be done about the amount of TV those two yobs watch." She pointed her thumb towards the living room. "It's sick. They're gonna end up with no brains. And Sadie has potential."

"What about Garth?"

"I think it's too late for him already." Emma grinned.

Frank chuckled. "I'll go up and see how your mother's doing. Nice job on the sandwiches, Em. Don't forget to make one for yourself."

"Yeah, Dad. Would you please tell the zombies their lunch is ready? I'm not giving it to them in front of the tube."

Frank scooped up his other two children and placed them where Emma wanted them.

"Mummy wet her pants." Sadie's eyes were big and she wasn't smiling.

Frank felt the bottom slip out—a shift, that freed his insides, tossed them every which way. He looked at Emma, who busied herself at the sink.

"Eat the sandwiches your sister made for you. I'll go on up and see your mum."

"I don't think Mummy wants to be disturbed right now, Daddy," Sadie said.

"Well, maybe she'll make an exception for me. Now, what do you say to Emma for making such a nice lunch?"

"Thank you very much for the sandwich, Em," Sadie said.

Frank kissed his younger daughter as he left the kitchen.

Denise lay awake on the bed in her terry towel robe. She had showered and her long wet hair was fanned out around her face like seaweed on the pillow. She didn't look at her husband when he entered the room.

Frank got a towel, laid it gently under her head and switched pillows on her. The one she had been lying on was soaking wet. Her face was puffy and bruised looking as though she had beaten herself up.

"Oh God, Frank, what must our children think of me?"

Frank couldn't think of a single thing to say so he put his arms around her and she let loose with a barrage of tears. Her hair smelled like apples, the same as it had the first time he had been close enough to notice. He had seen her then as filled with light, knowable. She had put old fears to rest. He denied for years that she had conjured up new ones that he hadn't known before.

He handed her some Kleenex now and waited.

"Do you hate me, Frank?"

"No, I don't hate you. I'm worried about you and I'm worried about our family, but I could never hate you."

They sounded like old words to Frank, used words that should have been thrown out with yesterday's garbage. But he didn't want to upset her, he didn't feel up to it. He hoped she wouldn't ask him if he loved her.

In the beginning, their conflicts had erupted and resolved themselves, securely fastened within the boundaries of their love. But as the years went by, those boundaries quivered and thinned; words and actions could bust clear through and fly around out there, testing the waters of a vast loneliness.

"Do you still love me, Frank?"

"Yes." He didn't pretty it up and he could see his doubts on her face, but it was the best he could do.

She stopped crying. "I'll go back to the hospital, Frank. Will you help me?"

"Of course." He kissed her on the temple as he got up to leave. "See if you can sleep awhile and I'll try and have it worked out by the time you wake up."

"Thanks." She sighed and laid down her head.

Frank was enjoying her absence in a way. The house was easier without her. It took a little getting used to, not trying to keep everyone quiet, talking in whispers. It was noisier, healthier. And Emma was old enough now that he probably wouldn't need to get Uncle Bosco to come from Regina to help with the kids. Gus would be happy to help out if it came to that. Poor Gus. He still seemed a little wobbly after the events of last Sunday.

Frank carried his coffee outside to a bench in the yard of the police station. New blades of grass poked through the matted lawn and a green sheen attached itself to the Manitoba Maples. The sun warmed a patch big enough for one person on the park bench.

Was there any way in the world that Denise would be able to turn her life around? Frank doubted it—she had tried on other occasions. He would be here for her again this time, but he didn't know if he could go on this way indefinitely. It was wearing him down.

He thought about Audrey, his girlfriend from high school days. They'd had a brief dalliance two summers ago. He wasn't proud of that, but not ashamed either. How had Audrey put it? Old business, something like that. Not to be worried about. Amazingly enough, he hadn't worried.

He admired the way she had just taken off. He didn't even wish he'd gone with her. It wasn't Audrey he wanted.

Frank couldn't let go of a thin shred of hope. Maybe some day he and Denise would do that—take off. Maybe on a motorcycle. When the kids were grown and he'd saved some money they could do it.

A squirrel approached; it was fat and fearless. Frank had nothing to offer.

He figured he wasn't cut out to be happy. Even when things were going well, like when Denise went for a period without drinking, he felt that he wasn't really inside of his life. Oh, he noticed the spring air and even felt an inkling of excitement at the change in the season. But it was tempered with something. There was a giant "if only" hanging over his head. If only I could really be here so I could smell that air and feel that excitement. I know it's good but it doesn't penetrate to the soul of me. Frank feared for his soul. He thought maybe it was lost.

What if Denise managed a new start and he was the one to let everyone down?

Frank apologized to the squirrel.

A wave of hopelessness washed over him. They weren't going to be taking a trip to anywhere. It was too late for motorcycles, maybe even motor homes.

He went back to his office, avoiding the main lobby. He didn't want to hobnob with the group of boisterous uniformed cops behind the reception counter.

The clock on the wall in his office told him he should be getting home soon. He couldn't put so much responsibility on Emma. Frank sat down at his desk and opened the rain barrel baby file. The mystery of the baby was very likely unsolvable. A week had already gone by since Gus had found her. Frank went over the facts of the case, forcing himself not to speculate. Just the facts.

The baby had lived outside of the womb. She was born alive approximately thirty-three weeks after conception and she died minutes later. She had breathed the air but had not tasted her mother's milk. Frank thought a baby would be bigger at eight months; she was so small. The birth and death occurred last fall. And as Gus suspected, the tiny girl wintered in the rain barrel.

It was a very small comfort that she was smothered before being dropped into the cold water. At least she didn't drown. Frank imagined drowning to be the worst death of all.

One last fact glared up at him from the medical examiner's report. The baby had been HIV-positive.

The only fingerprints on the barrel and its coverings were Gus' and Greta's. The same with the ladder and other items that could have been used to climb up on.

Fred Staples, one of the detective sergeants who worked under Frank, had checked with every hospital in the province for records of slightly premature babies born during the period in question. Nothing connected.

Frank phoned Fred to see if he was in. He was, so Frank asked him to drop by his office.

"The way I see it, Fred, there are three possibilities." Frank counted them off on his fingers. "One, the baby came from further afield than Manitoba; two, she was born outside a hospital; or three, she slipped through the cracks at a hospital within the province."

Fred stood at attention in front of the desk. Frank wished he wouldn't do that. Frank stood up and moved to the window where the late afternoon sun warmed the cold glass.

"I'd been thinking along the same lines," Fred said. "And I'm inclined to think that possibility number two may be the ticket: born outside of a hospital."

"In which case we're pretty much out of luck, aren't we?" Frank rattled the change in his pocket. "This may just end up being a really sad story that we can do nothing about. I mean, even if we found the mother that did this, what good would it do? She's pretty much got a death sentence anyway. The baby was HIV-positive, so she must be too, mustn't she?"

"She should be taken to task, sir."

Frank sighed. He didn't want to take anyone to task. And he wished Fred wouldn't call him sir. He'd asked him not to, but Fred couldn't seem to help it.

"Let's check hospitals in north Ontario and south Saskatchewan and then I think we may as well let it go," Frank said.

"I'll get on that right away, sir." Fred spun around on his heel. Frank wouldn't have been surprised if he'd saluted or if he'd continued spinning, clear around till he was facing the same way he'd started.

"How's Frances?" Frank asked before Fred closed the door.

He poked his head back in. "Fine, thanks, sir, I guess."

Frank had hoped that Fred's new wife would help loosen him up some, but so far there had been no evidence of it.

Frank sat down in his ergonomically correct chair. His ankles ached for no good reason. He worked for a few minutes trying to clear at least one item from his desk. It was a request from one of his sergeants for a transfer, out of Frank's division. He wondered if it had anything to do with him.

Reason for Transfer: Desire for change.

That didn't tell him much.

Frank set it aside. There was so much paperwork. His job now seemed to be mainly paperwork. And he didn't feel like doing it; he never felt like doing it.

So he opened his second from top drawer and dragged the soft woolen contents from their hiding spot over to his lap. He found his place and began to knit. Frank wasn't sure yet what he was building. The wool was blue, an irresistible blue. There was a ways to go before he had to decide on a particular item.

Just fifteen minutes and then he would go home and give Emma a break.

CHAPTER 6
1956

"It kinda goes to me," the kid says and the saleslady laughs.

The mother has taken her downtown to buy something to wear for the first day of grade one. The dress is covered with butterflies and the kid loves it. A tiny net butterfly perches on the black velvet belt. Perfect.

Suddenly, in the middle of the new clothes, her mother disappears and ladies hover. They know all about it.

"Your mummy had to go for a ride, dear, in a car. These nice men will take you home. They know where you live."

"Can't I go with my mum?" the kid asks.

"Don't worry, honey. She'll be fine. There was just a little misunderstanding. I'm sure that's all it was. You go now with the nice men."

"What about the butterfly dress?" she asks.

"We'll keep it for you, dear, and you and your mum can come back for it."

An ice-cream cone appears in her hand and she rides home in a black and white car. The nice men are police.

They don't go back for the dress and a few days later a girl in her class wears it to school.

The kid cries, right there at her desk.

"What is it, dear?" the teacher asks. "What's wrong?"

But she can't say. She doesn't have the words to describe what's wrong. She can't even make a start.

CHAPTER 7
The Present

Emma kissed her pillow. Then she kissed her arm. She hadn't kissed a boy yet, but she hoped to soon.

Emma and Delia had explored each other's bodies pretty thoroughly, but they hadn't kissed. They hadn't wanted to.

Delia had given her the idea about practising on her pillow and on her arm. She had already kissed a boy and said it was really great. Emma believed her and couldn't wait. She wished her arm didn't have quite so many freckles.

She had a picture of the boy she wanted to kiss: Donald Griffiths. He was in her home room at school and when they'd had their pictures taken she had asked him for one. Her bravery had astonished her. She thought she camouflaged her desire fairly well in the hubbub of laughter and trading going on when their school pictures arrived.

He didn't seem surprised, just smiled and said, "Sure. Can I have one of you too?"

Emma suspected he had asked just to be polite but she gave him one and wrote on the back: To Donald, from Emma Foote. He didn't write anything on the back of his, which was a little disappointing, but she hadn't wanted to force him into anything further.

Emma loved Donald and thought about him all the time. Delia knew how she felt and was pretty good at encouraging her and cheering her up when she felt there was no hope.

Emma had decided that she would let Donald touch her breasts after they had kissed several times on different occasions. That's if he wanted to. Her breasts weren't very big but he might want to anyway. She figured it was okay to go that far and wanted badly for it to happen. She was pretty definite about not doing anything more than that though.

What she had done with Delia didn't really count. It was more for educational purposes.

And what she did on her own was something else entirely. She did that now as she imagined kissing Donald. She kissed his picture but that didn't work as well as her arm. It was too flat and smooth.

Afterwards she thought about her science project. Her idea was to build a volcano that would actually erupt. It wouldn't be easy but she figured it was something she could pull off. Maybe her dad would help. Maybe Donald would help! He was a bit of a science geek.

If only my breasts were a little larger, Emma thought, and pushed them together, making a feeble cleavage. It hurt, so she let go and turned sideways to look in the mirror. Oh well, at least I don't have wiener breasts. That was Delia's expression. Her mum had wiener breasts, so Delia figured she was doomed to the same fate. They weren't wieners yet, though. It was more of an older woman's thing.

CHAPTER 8

Ivy Grace sat on a park bench outside The Forks Market. She faced the river and beyond it the beauty of Old Saint Boniface, but her eyes didn't take it in; she was contemplating her next move. For two years, four months, one day, fifteen hours and—she looked at her watch—fourteen minutes, she had been working on her plan, and it was falling into place. Actually, she had begun long before that, she just hadn't realized it. She'd known she was working towards something, probably since the day she walked out of her mother's house twenty-nine years ago, but she hadn't known what. It hadn't come clear all at once, far from it.

But now, she had completed the first steps and it was time to move on. She thought back to the Saturday morning, two and a third years ago, when she had gotten started. In the practical sense.

On that day, when the plan shaped itself in her mind, Ivy had stood admiring herself, the result of her efforts, in her full-length mirror. She smiled slowly, worked at it. She knew the smile was important.

Her notebook had lain open on her desk and she'd gone over to consult it: Admire self in mirror. Okay. Practise smiling so it includes eyes. Okay.

Next came something she didn't like to do. Pray. It was important. She would be lost without her prayers, without whatever it was she prayed to, telling her what to write in her notebook. It was just that she hated the process. She wished she could just open the book each day and find the words neatly in place.

Praying hurt—her stomach mostly. And sometimes it made her throat ache. The trouble was, sometimes the hurt wouldn't go away but would stick with her all day. Even into the night.

Her sleep used to be as deep and black as death when she had been seeing Dr. Braun. He gave her pills—pills for this, pills for that. They worked, but she didn't like the man. She had given him up and with him her sound sleeps.

It had to be done, so she did it. Knelt by her bed, laid her head on the soft sweet scent of the goose down comforter, carefully, so as not to disturb her hair or face. It didn't take long for the words to come. They started and ended abruptly. The voice that spoke to her was female, familiar, but nothing she could tie a name to. So she made one up. Gruck. It fit. Sometimes she thought of it simply as G. That morning, as always, G gave her the words to get her through that day and part way through the next.

Ivy wrote the words from G with pencil in backhand till she filled one page of her notebook. Then she went back to where she began, to double check her next move. The writing was almost unreadable: Scout out a man, any man.

Sometimes she wished Gruck would give her more complete information, the hows and the wheres. But that part was left up to her. Ivy supposed there was a reason for this, so didn't question it, just wished sometimes it could be easier.

For instance, it was awfully early in the day to find a man in the sense that she knew G wanted her to find one. But she would have to try. It was for the men that she took such care with her appearance. G insisted on it.

The bars weren't open yet. The supermarket, she supposed, and if that didn't work she could try an art gallery or a museum.

She erased the sentence declaring the task at hand.

At the Safeway things went much more easily than she had anticipated.

"I never know how to pick a cantaloupe," she said, holding the round fruit helplessly in both hands, squeezing gently.

"Here. Let me help." The man jumped in as she knew he would. He had a white puppy tucked into his coat.

The rest was easy, except for the part where she insisted that he not use any protection. That had put him off, just for a bit, and he'd thought she was strange.

Well, she was strange and she was also fixin' to die. That was the way she liked to think of it, to phrase it.

Now, all this time later, she had what she had been looking for and it was time for the next step. Frank Foote didn't know it, but he was the key.

Ivy stood up and gazed upon the river that had drawn her there in the first place. Across the water the spires of Saint Boniface caught her eye. So sharp. It distressed her to look at them, but at the same time, she couldn't tear her eyes away.

CHAPTER 9

Frank stopped in to see Greta on his way home from work on Monday to tell her that there was no news about the rain barrel baby. She didn't seem to care. In fact, she didn't want to talk about that baby at all.

"Would you like a glass of wine, Frank? I've got some open."

Frank didn't like to drink on weekdays if he could help it. "That'd be nice," he said.

He could celebrate not having to answer the questions of a more inquisitive person, questions like: was she born dead; did she drown; did she suffer much?

Greta placed a glass of Italian red in Frank's hand and he settled himself across from her at the kitchen table.

There were at least one hundred cherry tarts cooling on racks right there in front of him. He would have loved to scarf down a couple of those, but he knew they were for business purposes and didn't like to ask. Surely she would offer! Or maybe she made the exact number required and there was no room for casual munching.

"Did I tell you that my daughter is a nurse?" Greta asked.

"Pardon me?"

"My daughter. She's a nurse. She got in touch with me a few years back." Greta's face was shiny and red, as though she had scrubbed it too hard.

"I filled out a form ages ago at the Provincial Registry, you know, in case my daughter was looking for me? My baby girl? Nothing ever came of that, but she found me on her own."

"You met her then? You saw her?" Frank wondered if Greta was a booze hound.

"Well, no, I didn't. It was a bit of a disappointment really. She wrote me a letter, but she didn't want to see me. The letter was on River City Health Centre stationery. That's where she said she was a nurse. She didn't want me to know where she lived, I guess."

The cat, Ailsa, wound her way around Frank's legs. He reached down to scratch her forehead.

"Her last name is Mallet," Greta said. "And her first name's still Jane. I was pleased about that. They must have thought it was good enough to keep. I phoned every Mallet in the phone book, but none of them knew what I was talking about."

"How did she find you if she didn't sign on at the Registry?" Frank stroked Ailsa's soft gray fur. The cat stood with her two front paws on Frank's thigh.

"Simple," Greta said. "In 1968, when I gave her away, my name was written on the adoption order. She must have seen it at some point. And I'm in the phone book.

"I phoned River City looking for her. But they told me that they didn't have a nurse there named Jane Mallet. I guess she lied to me about that."

Greta drank greedily from her glass and poured herself some more. Frank was just approaching his first sip.

"I believe she is a nurse, though," Greta said. "Why would she make that up? She probably just didn't want me to know how to get in touch with her. I mean, she would hate me, wouldn't she?"

Frank drank.

"I tried every hospital in town. No one had a Nurse Jane Mallet. But she could be a private nurse, couldn't she? Or something like that."

"Yes," Frank said. "Or she could be in another city."

"Yeah. Something like that. She got in touch once more, just last year, by phone that time. Just wanted me to know she was happily married and still successfully employed, I guess. That was about all she talked about."

"Is she still going by the name Mallet?" Frank asked.

"I think so. That's what she called herself. Jane Mallet."

Greta drained her glass again and watched Frank from under heavy eyelids. "She talked kinda funny, Jane did."

"What do you mean, funny?" Frank asked. And what's the matter with your eyes? But he kept that question to himself. He didn't want her bursting into tears. Frank was pretty sure she was swacked, even though her words came out crisp around the edges.

"Sort of slow," Greta said. "As though she had to think really hard about each word."

She got up from the table and walked around behind Frank. She leaned into him until his head was cushioned between her breasts.

One for each ear. He remembered what it had been like to bury his face in those breasts. It seemed like a hundred years ago. Greta's breasts were far and away the biggest ones he'd ever dealt with. Pneumatic. He'd enjoyed it very much, he recalled now.

"Frank, would you like to have sex with me?" Crisp words. She caressed his hair with gentle fingers.

Shudders ran through him and he leapt to his feet startling Ailsa and knocking over his chair. He had very little room to manoeuvre.

"I'm sure that'd be very nice, Greta, but I'm married and I should get going."

She laughed.

Frank stared at her body inside her summer dress.

She undid a few buttons.

Frank reached out and then stopped. "I can't do this."

She took his hand and covered her face with it.

"You have beautiful hands, Frank. I love big hands."

She ran her tongue the length of his middle finger and took it in her mouth. She sucked it gently to the last knuckle holding his eyes all the while.

He groaned and reached out with his other hand to touch her hair. It was so soft. Rain water. Tinged with…

"Oh, God, Greta. I'd really love to, but I can't." He pulled his hand away. "I gotta go now. I'll be in touch."

She smiled and so did he.

As he walked down the street toward his house he felt her mouth swallowing his finger. He looked at it. It was still wet. It felt different from his other fingers. He pictured licking her and biting her and fucking her till he was spent. He loved that she had looked at him. Denise always looked away.

It would have been so easy. But the consequences could be anything but. Greta was unpredictable. He imagined her phoning, sending letters, befriending Denise and threatening to tell her if he didn't fuck her more often or let her act out her wildest fantasies in his presence.

Frank chuckled to himself. He liked that Greta wanted him and he was pleased with himself for turning her down.

He'd run out of there so fast there'd been no chance for her to offer him a cherry tart for the road. Oh well. He was pretty sure there was a Sara Lee cake in the freezer at home. That'd have to do.

CHAPTER 10

Emma and Delia smoked cigars by the river. Emma had stolen hers from Frank. He kept a small stash in the freezer and enjoyed one now and then in the summer. Delia bought hers at Shoppers Drug Mart. She looked older than her fourteen years and was sometimes able to buy tobacco, depending who was working the till. Today she'd been lucky.

Emma's cigar was made from pipe tobacco and smelled a lot better than Delia's, which stank like a regular stogie. They were careful not to breathe in the smoke. Emma had inhaled once, a Cuban cigar stolen from Delia's mother's boyfriend, and she had coughed for half an hour solid, and then intermittently for an hour after that.

She wanted to tell Delia about her mother wetting her pants, but she couldn't. She had tried once to talk about her mum's drunkenness with her friend, but Delia had laughed and Emma had wished more than anything that she hadn't bothered. The laughter came as a complete surprise to her. It had made her feel very alone.

So they talked about boys. Donald in particular and a boy named Vince that Delia yearned for.

"Okay, first we have to fix it so that Donald and Vince become friends," Delia said, "so that they hang around together. It'll be easier for us if they do."

"Then they'll pursue us," Emma said. "Overcoming all kinds of obstacles, like other guys who will also be madly in love with us. Especially me."

"No. Especially me." Delia pushed Emma.

"No, me." Emma pushed back. "Vince's parents will go out of town and Donald will stay at his house." She puffed thoughtfully on her sweet-smelling cigar.

"And they'll invite us over for the night," Delia said. "You'll say you're sleeping at my house and I'll say I'm sleeping at yours and we'll stay with Vince and Donald all night long."

"Donald and Vince."

"Vince and Donald."

"Donald and Vinnie."

"Vince and Don-boy."

"Shut up!"

"You started it!"

"We'll have dinner and listen to Sheryl Crow," Emma said.

"Who's gonna cook?"

"We'll order in. From Santa Lucia. They make great dinners. We can pretend to the guys that we did the cooking so they'll wanna marry us."

"I don't wanna marry anybody." Delia blew a perfect smoke ring.

"I do," Emma said. "After supper we'll retire to two separate bedrooms."

"Retire?"

"Yeah. Me and Donald will go to Vince's parents' bedroom and you and Vince will go to his bedroom."

"I wanna use the parents' room. It'll be nicer."

"No. Sorry. Dibs on the parents' room. Anyway, Vince'll want to show you his stuff, like his model airplanes and his Pamela Lee collection."

"Fuck off! He won't have stuff like that. He'll have like, knives and bullets and stuff."

"I'll talk to Donald." Emma tried a smoke ring but, as usual, it didn't come close. "He'll listen and he'll tell me his secrets and I'll understand. And we'll kiss and talk till morning comes. I won't smoke any cigars that day."

"Won't you be having sex?"

"No."

"I'm pretty sure I will be," Delia said. "I think Vince has had shitloads of experience with women. He's probably been seduced by one of his mother's friends, I figure. He'll be the one to show me how to have sex. God, I am so ready for this."

Emma was so not ready for that yet. On this first occasion it would just be kisses.

When their cigars were finished Emma and Delia followed the path up from the river and headed for the 7-Eleven for food and drink to get rid of the horrible tastes in their mouths.

That night Emma gazed out her open window at the bright back garden. The moon shone in such a way that the shadows fell elsewhere. A rabbit sat in the centre of the yard, perfectly still. It could have been made of glass. Emma made a sound at the window, just a breath really, but enough to alert the rabbit. It didn't turn its head to see her, or run away to avoid her. It stayed the same except for a quiver. Her sound was too small to cause more than that, but too big for things to stay as they were. The rabbit was in limbo. Purgatory.

Emma shivered. The rabbit's fear was for its life. What else was there? It didn't have to worry about its breasts not growing or having stared too long at a boy that it wanted to kiss. All it had to worry about was being killed.

"Don't worry, little rabbit," Emma called. "I'm not gonna hurt ya."

A car door clicked shut at the same time that Emma spoke. She didn't hear it, but the rabbit did and hopped into the darkness under the almond hedge.

CHAPTER 11
1958

He's eleven to her seven, a big kid. He leans against the apple tree and makes room against his chest for her small and trembly body. The ache in her neck is the worst. She can hardly move her head.

Ray holds her gently and rests his chin on her tangled hair. He sings a song from the radio. Words of love. Buddy Holly is his favourite. She feels light-headed, disconnected, but the fear in her gut begins to subside.

The scent of apple blossom fills the air, mingled with the unbearably sweet fragrance of the plum. Ray strokes her hair. The sunlight slants through the new leaves and hurts her eyes, but it's a good hurt. Not like when her mother shakes her.

A few doors down a push mower clatters quietly through its task. "Just the boulevard, Ronnie, dear," a mother calls. "The rest of the grass doesn't really need it yet."

Ray laughs. A kid who cuts the lawn before it really needs it.

She feels safe with Ray on this evening in spring, cool breeze on her hot face. She trusts him; he's her brother.

CHAPTER 12
The Present

In the dream his love moved inside her. He was her husband. And her friend.

"I've missed you so much," he says and kisses her face.
He offers her cherry pound cake and she bites into the sweet dense pastry.

"Mmm," Denise Foote murmured in her sleep.

He sits next to her and when she moves away he follows.
She longs to be desired, even if it's only because of her hair and smooth skin. She's nineteen.

Denise woke up.

The loss of sharing her kisses felt like the biggest loss of her life. She saw now that it might be wrong to feel that way. Wrong-headed, as her mother used to say. It might not be right, but it was true. How can something true be wrong? Easy. It was true that she loved one of her children less than the other two and that couldn't be right, could it?

Denise closed her eyes and felt Sadie insinuating herself between her and Frank in their bed. This morning? No. Nowhere near this morning. Denise had pressed her face into Sadie's hair and smelled sweet, warm grass. She kissed the spot where her daughter's soft brown hair parted and Sadie had nestled up against her.

"Help, Nurse!"

Denise heard the call from the next bed but she couldn't rouse herself to help. A terrible smell filled her whole world and what seemed like hours passed.

"What is it, Mrs. Blagden?" the nurse finally asked. "What do you need?"

"I think I've pooped in the bed." Mrs. Blagden started to cry.

"Yes, I think you have," said the nurse. "Just hang on and we'll get you cleaned up."

Denise wanted back inside her dream or back into bed with Sadie. She wanted to think about kisses some more. Not about the woman in the next bed. It could have been her.

The day at the mall came back to her. Maybe it was a dream. She had been drunk, just a little. Only Frank and Emma would have realized it. The rest of the world didn't know her well enough to mark the changes in her when she drank. It had been so much easier when Emma was younger and hadn't taken issue with everything. All the time. Being a secret drunk was hard work but Denise thought she was pretty good at it. Lying was second nature to her.

"Hi, Denise. How's it goin'?" The soft voice had startled her while she shopped and her hand flew to her chest. Little bottles rolled.

"Jesus!" she said, and looked into the pale eyes of someone she realized she was supposed to know. Someone from the neighbourhood?

Another man, this one wearing an apron, busied himself at her feet cleaning up the mess.

"Smirnoff, eh?" The stranger's voice rasped through thin lips.

Who was this guy?

"In the wee bottles," he said. "An old lady's trick. Expensive habit. I guess you think you're fooling someone."

"Who are you?" Denise spluttered.

The flat face smirked.

She couldn't remember for a moment if she'd finished her business there but it no longer mattered. She had run from the liquor store.

Denise shuddered now as she remembered. It was no dream. She recalled too where she had seen the man before. He had been a member of a group she had belonged to once when she was trying to quit drinking. He'd been bossy and arrogant and one of the reasons she'd quit going. That was the trouble with groups. They had people in them.

She hadn't stopped running till she'd reached her car and locked the doors. She panted like a dog on a hot day, bathed in sweat and self-loathing. So little had actually happened. That was the worst knowledge of all.

Something stank. After a few minutes she had raised her head from the steering wheel, breathed in deeply and realized to her horror that she had wet her pants.

She groaned aloud now as she heard the nurse fussing over Mrs. Blagden.

"Everything all right, Mrs. Foote?" the night nurse asked.

"Terrific, thanks."

CHAPTER 13

Greta Bower is mowing her lawn in the early morning and Gus goes over to have a word with her. The sound of the gas mower roars through his chest and it astonishes him that anyone could be so insensitive. It's barely dawn!

As he approaches Greta, her pretty face turns into the head of the woman he saw in front of Frank's place the other night. She is all sunglasses and red lips. Only this time, the lips open in a stiff smile to reveal a row of broken teeth, bluish in colour. The half-teeth move, and on closer inspection Gus sees that tiny blue worms slither over the jagged surfaces. The heads of the worms are black, and the creatures have teeth of their own, sharp teeth that gnaw at their own blue bodies.

Gus jerked himself awake before the dream went further. He put on a coat and shuffled out to his front porch to breathe some fresh air and try to forget the terrible picture left in his brain. He had been reading about Blue-footed Boobies earlier in the day and suspected that was why his dream worms were two-toned. And Greta didn't even own a lawn mower. She let her yard go to rack and ruin all in the name of something that Gus couldn't remember.

"Howdy, Gus," Frank called over from his own front porch next door.

"Frank. Just the man," Gus whispered as loudly as he could. "Get yourself over here, why don't ya, so we don't have to shout and wake up the whole neighbourhood?"

Frank chuckled. "I don't think I've ever heard anyone whisper as loud as you, Gus. When it gets to be that loud most folks would turn it into talking." He sauntered over to where Gus leaned on the railing, and looked up at him.

"Let's have a drink," Gus said. "I don't think Greta quite wiped out that bottle of brandy."

"Not for me, thanks, Gus, but I'll sit with you a while." He climbed the steps to the porch and plunked himself down on one of the two straight-backed chairs.

"Do you want to go inside, Frank? It's pretty chilly out here."

Both men wore winter parkas with the hoods up.

"No, I've got enough clothes on. I was suffocating indoors."

"How 'bout some cocoa?"

"No thanks, Gus, but you go ahead. The caffeine in the chocolate keeps me awake and I sure don't need that."

"Water?"

"No thanks, I'm fine as is. If I drink water after supper, then I end up going to the bathroom all night long."

"Jesus, Frank. What the hell are you going to be like when you get to be my age?"

Gus sat down in the other chair.

"Trouble sleeping?" he asked.

"Yeah, most nights, I guess."

"Is it the baby in the rain barrel, Frank?"

"No, Gus. Awful as that is, it's not what keeps me awake nights."

Gus was quiet and Frank was grateful to him for not pushing. He wasn't sure if he wanted to talk or not. Maybe just sitting a while would be good. They could start with sitting anyway.

Venus was so bright it looked like more than a star. Frank stared at it till his eyes lost their focus and the light became fantastic. He pulled himself back.

"How are you getting along with it, Gus? The baby, I mean."

"Well, I must say, it's not an easy thing to put behind me. I think about it a lot and dream about it a bit, but it's not as bad as it was."

"I wake up after three hours," Frank said, "and then I can't get back to sleep. It's always just three hours. I don't think I can live on that." He looked over at Gus. "Sometimes I think I'm going insane."

"Jeez, Frank, that sounds horrible. All I can say is that I'm sure it'll eventually pass. I know that doesn't do you much good right now. I went through a similar bout once. Around the time they forced me to retire. I used to sit out here for hours—thank God it was summer—and watch the sun come up. But it wasn't fun, I'll tell ya. I wasn't really worried about anything in particular. I just couldn't come up with anything good to think about. And my mind was too jittery for sleep."

Gus put his feet up on the wooden railing that ran around the porch.

"I should put something more comfortable out here to sit on," he said. "Something that would accommodate a man's legs and feet. In the daytime," he went on, "I would roam around the house and yard lookin' at things that needed doing that I didn't have the energy for. I swear to God, I broke down and wept more than once, scared the bejesus out of Irma. I felt like my life was over, except I hadn't died. And then I got better. Just like that."

"I wish I could have met Irma." Frank stretched out his long legs and rested his feet on the rail next to Gus'.

"I wish you could've too, Frank. She was great."

"I knew her to see her. I knew who you both were way back when. She was pretty. I remember thinking she was pretty."

"That she was, Frank. That she was."

Frank was worried about his kids. He worried a lot, especially about Em, who seemed so old somehow. He wondered if they shouldn't have named her Emma. Maybe a little girl's name like Amy or Tracy would have been better.

Morning had come early that day to the Foote house, with Sadie leaping into action at the first sign of light. Her mother's absence hadn't made her any less joyful. She sat in her yellow pajamas atop Frank, who was trying to stay inside his daydream for a few moments longer. Or maybe he was asleep. Anyway, it was a marvelous dream in which he was ordered by some higher law to have sex with Audrey. They were in the desert at night, under a million stars like in that old Eagles song. They were sometimes their young selves and sometimes their present selves. They gazed into each other's faces and at some points, if the concentration was strong enough, they could move smoothly into each other's consciousnesses.

"Good morning, Daddy."

"Good morning, Sadie dear." Frank could hear the television. Garth must be up too.

"Time to jump up," Sadie said.

Frank smiled. "Well, I don't think I'll be doing much jumping this morning, but I guess it is time I was up."

He got out of bed slowly, feeling a tight lump of pain between his shoulders. He pictured himself with ice for his neck, a huge cup of coffee and the newspaper, heading straight back to bed.

When he looked in on Emma he saw her elfin face turned inward to a worrisome dream. Sadie started towards her, but Frank swept her up and away to her morning rituals, and closed the door so his other daughter might sleep on. His back was killing him so he took one of the anti-inflammatory pills that Dr. Kowalski had prescribed. They were pretty good and there wasn't going to be time for ice.

Sadie was soon set up beside her brother in front of the TV with a bowl of cereal. Garth had already eaten, judging from the small array of items laid out in front of him. There was an expertly opened empty tin of sardines, a spoon, and a glass of chocolate milk. Frank had to repress his gagging instinct, but admired his son for his expertise with the key on the sardine tin. Not a ripped finger in sight.

"Howdy, Garth."

"Hi, Dad." Garth's eyes didn't leave the TV. It was an *Avengers* rerun.

"Mrs. Peel," said Sadie happily as she settled in beside Garth.

"Yup, that's her all right." Frank smiled down at his kids. "Don't forget to clean up your breakfast stuff, Garth, before Hugh gets too interested."

Hugh was their one-year-old cat who sat in a corner of the room staring at the sardine tin.

Frank made coffee and called the hospital. Denise had had a quiet night. He went back upstairs and looked in on Emma, who was now sitting at her computer in her pajamas.

"Hi, Em. How's it goin'?"

She erased the screen. "Hi, Dad. Pretty good, I guess. I have to do a science project and I don't know where to start."

"Science project, eh? Hmm." Frank paused so his daughter would think he was giving this some serious thought. He also knew that she knew better. She was impossible to lie to, even silently. He supposed this was a good thing. It kept him on his toes.

"I'm thinkin' about a volcano," she said.

"That's a good idea. It could erupt."

"Yeah. That's what I was thinkin'."

"Would you mind coming downstairs for a minute, Em, so I can speak to all of you at the same time?"

"What about?"

"Well, your mum and stuff."

Emma sighed as she put on her robe and slippers to accompany Frank downstairs.

"My head aches, Gus," Frank said now, staring straight ahead into the darkness. "It aches all the time."

Gus grunted companionably and said, "How're those kids of yours?"

Frank turned to look at his neighbour. "God, I'm so worried about them, Gus. Em seems so old and Garth can't take his eyes off the TV and all they ever seem to want to talk about is death. I don't think I can bear it if Sadie ever gets less happy than she was first thing this morning. And it's got to happen. It's happening right now and I don't feel as though I'm up to it."

Gus reached over and touched Frank's shoulder. "It's hard being a father, Frank. And you're doin' good. I know you are. You're doin' real good, in fact."

"Do you really think so, Gus? You're not just saying that?"

Frank recalled how adrift he had felt that morning as he gently pushed Emma ahead of him into the living room, where he turned off the TV in an effort to get everyone's attention.

"Hey!" shouted Garth.

"Quiet," Frank said. "I want your serious attention for a few minutes."

Emma and Sadie both looked at Garth to see how he would react to missing the resolution of Mrs. Peel and Steed's latest adventure.

"It's okay," he said. "I've already seen this one."

"Good," said Frank. "Okay. I'm not sure how long your mum is going to be away this time, but it could be for longer than a few days. I've decided not to ask Bosco to come and stay with us and we'll just see how it goes. We'll see if we can manage, the four of us."

"Who's Bosco?" Sadie asked.

"Oh. I guess you don't remember him, Sadie. It's been a couple of years. He stayed with us the last time your mum went away. He's your great uncle, my dad's brother."

"Who's your dad?" Sadie asked.

"My dad is your grandfather, but he's been dead for several years, so you never got to meet him."

"How did he die?" Garth asked.

"He had a heart attack," Frank said.

"Massive?"

"Yeah. I guess so. He died from it, so it must have been pretty big."

"Did he die quickly?" Emma asked.

"Yeah," Frank sighed. "I don't think he knew what hit him."

"Where's Mummy?" Sadie climbed onto Frank's lap and he was glad to change the subject back to the even more difficult one of Denise's absence.

"Well, Sadie, Mummy hasn't been feeling very well, so she's gone into the hospital for a rest."

"To the Chemical Withdrawal Unit?" Garth asked.

"Well…yes."

"Is it because she wet her pants?" Sadie asked.

Frank pictured his grown-up daughter at a support group in the twenty-first century, sharing, "My mother wet her pants when I was six. I never got over it."

"Well, that's part of it, I guess," he said. "Anyway, she misses you all very much and trusts that we'll all be able to take care of ourselves. And she asked me to ask Gus, next door, to keep an eye on us too."

Emma made a kind of huffy sound at this point.

"Em, I know you feel you don't need taking care of, but Sadie and Garth do. With my work and your school, we'll be busy, you and me. We should be really grateful to Gus for being such a generous neighbour. Maybe he'd help you with your science project. He's real good at stuff like that."

"I don't need taking care of," Garth said.

"I do, Daddy," Sadie said.

"I know you do, Sweetie, and you're going to be taken care of real well."

"I'm not old enough to take care of myself yet." Sadie looked at her father with fear on her little face.

A thin outline of pain had settled itself around Frank's head and stayed there all day.

He turned to Gus now. "Thanks, Gus. You're a good neighbour and friend."

"Anytime, Frank. Anytime."

When Frank stood up to leave, Gus asked, "Have they buried the little gal yet?"

"Yes, they have. At Brookside Cemetery. In the children's section."

"Is there a marker for the grave?"

"Yeah, one of those white slabs. It says Jane on it. That's my fault, I guess. They wanted a name and that's the one I came up with."

"Jane's a beautiful name, Frank. That's one of my grandmothers' names."

Frank didn't mention to Gus that Jane was also the name of the baby Greta gave away twenty-seven years ago. It had seemed like a secret when she told him. That Jane had been on Frank's mind a lot. She was on his mind now as he trudged back across the yard to his own house.

And Gus didn't tell Frank about the woman in the car, although he started to once or twice. He decided that now wasn't the time. The poor guy had enough on his plate.

Gus stayed up. He'd had enough of sleep for one night if it was going to mean being frightened by images of evil women with rotten teeth. And he didn't have a job to get up for or a family to synchronize his meals or moods with.

The weight of Frank's woes saddened him and left him wondering how he could better help his friend. But alongside the sadness was a whir of energy that buoyed him up and he knew better than to question or ignore it. He saw the paling of the sky in the east and trusted with all his heart the good feeling and the new day.

CHAPTER 14

On Tuesday Frank knocked off work a little early and went home to work on his garage. And to see his kids. Just Emma and Sadie were home; Garth had stayed at school for soccer practice.

Frank had an idea involving Jane Mallet, the daughter Greta Bower had given up for adoption. It was a feeble hunch—no alarms were ringing—but it was a hunch nonetheless. And it was the only thing he had when it came to the rain barrel baby, so he supposed he should follow it up.

His arms were getting tired. He had been scraping old paint off his garage for only thirty minutes but he was ready to pack it in.

I must really be out of shape, he thought, if I can't even prepare my own garage for paint without feeling as though I'm going to have a major health episode of some kind.

Frank's hunch, as well as being feeble, seemed a little far-fetched, so he had kept quiet about it. He didn't share it with Detective Sergeant Fred Staples, or with his boss, Superintendent Ed Flagston. The official reason he gave himself was that he was grasping at straws, but there were other reasons swimming about in Frank's thoughts. Reasons that had to do with Fred's black and white way of seeing things, and his own tendency to hide the police manual under his mattress at times.

He didn't want to involve Greta unnecessarily. She seemed so emotionally frail to him. He supposed he could be making that up, casting himself in the role of protector to make up for all his failures.

He couldn't save Denise and worried that he was the root of her problems. She had seemed so…well…unalcoholic when he had first met her. She had been working hard to put herself through university. And she had done it—graduated with a degree in anthropology.

Her plan then was to work for awhile—she got a job with the provincial government in the archives—and then go back and get her master's degree. She wanted to go on archeological digs, research the past. She wanted to go to Egypt.

Denise hadn't wanted kids; she'd been definite about that. Frank had wanted them so badly he could taste it, but he wanted her, too, and figured she'd come around and get over her desire to travel the world looking for things that happened thousands of years ago.

She didn't come around, but she got pregnant by accident and Emma was born. Frank had been so afraid she would have an abortion that he lost thirty pounds. He thanked God for the Catholicism that had been drilled into Denise as a kid.

They had both agreed that Emma shouldn't be an only child and then, oddly, it had taken five years for Denise to become pregnant again.

She had been fairly well organized in her drinking. Never touching a drop when she was pregnant or breast feeding, but then going on binges. She usually managed to get supper on the table and the kids tended to, half-heartedly, but sometimes just barely. Frank had insisted on a mother's helper part of the time and had taken two fairly lengthy leaves of absence from his own job to help out at home. Denise's drinking had gotten worse since Sadie was weaned over five years ago.

Frank had suggested more than once that she try heading back to university for a course or two towards that once longed-for master's degree. But she didn't figure she could do both that and be a mother.

You combine being a mother and drinking like a wild woman! he had wanted to shout. You could substitute the courses for your benders. It would be easier! But he never had. He supposed the whole mess was his fault. He had wanted kids so badly. Surely that wasn't wrong, was it?

"Hi, Dad." It was Garth, smiling full tilt into the sun.

"Hi, Garth!" Frank came down off the step-ladder. "Do you want to help me scrape the garage?"

"No thanks."

Frank chuckled. "I don't blame you. It's a horrible job. How was soccer practice?"

"Okay, I guess."

Frank noticed that Garth's neck was dirty. "Maybe you should have a bath. What do you think?"

"No. I'm fine, thanks." Garth continued along into the house.

Frank wondered if Sadie's neck was also dirty. He'd have to check. And if Garth wasn't cleaned up at bedtime he'd make him take a bath and clean out the tub afterwards.

Frank sat down in a shady spot and leaned against the old wood of his garage.

Greta had been taking care of herself reasonably well for forty-two years. She had a hugely successful baking business and as for her drinking, Frank figured he was probably just overly sensitive to it because of Denise. But he didn't want Greta involved unless she had to be. She was so messy.

He also didn't want to embroil the mysterious Jane Mallet in something unless it became necessary. And he hadn't even met her yet. But it was time to find her; he had a feeling it wouldn't be hard. He could start with the River City Health Centre.

In the 1960s when a baby was adopted, the names of the birth parents were still put on the adoption order. A copy of this order was given to the adoptive parents if they wanted it. Frank had checked. Greta had told him as much, but he didn't put a lot of stock in what Greta said.

Frank pictured the adoption order filed in a shoe box of important papers high on a shelf in Mother Mallet's closet. And young Jane, snooping as children do, through the mysteries of her mother's fabrics and scents, for secrets better left alone.

Frank took off his shirt and used it to wipe the sweat from his eyes. It was too hot for this kind of work. He made a pillow out of his shirt and placed it behind his head. Now all he needed was a cold drink. He was going to have to have a shower before figuring out what to do about supper. Manual labour on such a hot day was a stupid idea. Frank felt as though he was full of stupid ideas.

Jane Mallet knew who her mother was. Frank didn't doubt that. Nurse and happy marriage stories aside, he believed the basic information that Greta had given him: her daughter had been in touch. But why? She hadn't wanted to get together with Greta, but she obviously knew where Greta lived if she had contacted her. That was a little odd.

Greta Bower was also a little odd and sometimes that ran in families. She was also a woman who had given away her child. Being given away was as good a reason as any for hating someone, Frank thought, for wanting to punish them. Perhaps Jane Mallet had placed her own dead baby in her mother's rain barrel as a form of twisted revenge.

Emma held the screen door for Sadie, who balanced a tray containing a frosty glass of lemonade and three chocolate chip cookies, fresh from the oven. She approached her father carefully and didn't spill a drop.

CHAPTER 15

In her dream, Ivy can't come clean. She showers and scrubs and showers again, but she can't rid herself of the dirt. It comes from within. She sullies the world with her presence. Everything she touches is tainted with her filth.

Ivy Grace collects things with points. Dull points as in those eraser tubes where you pull a string to reveal more of the rubber. Sharp points as in scissors and pencils honed to nothing. Paper clips. Keys. Bottles. Bobby pins. Ornaments. Knives. Forks. Garden tools. Wieners. Licorice whips.

There are a couple of criteria: they have to be longer than they are wide and they have to be under a specific length. If one end is narrower than the other it is a bonus but not a necessity.

She finds these things and hides them in a satchel along with a length of heavy twine and some duct tape.

She doesn't know why. It has something to do with the muddled Squeaks that she hears inside her head. The Squeaks come separately from the other voice, Gruck, the one that comes when she prays. The Squeaks lead her in directions that she isn't aware of till after the fact.

For example: the duct tape. Where has it come from? She sees herself placing it carefully with her bag of pointed objects. But she can't recall deciding she needed it or going to get it. The last thing she remembers is the Squeaks starting, and looking at her watch, she sees that was an hour and sixteen minutes ago. She has been lost inside the Squeaks for all that time and the result is a partially used roll of duct tape.

CHAPTER 16
1960

"Shut up!" the mother shouts. It gets quiet then, too quiet, and she calls for her son. "Ray," she calls. "Ray, come and see to your sister. The clumsy fool has fallen down the cellar stairs."

Ray comes running from his bedroom, dread in his heart. He thinks his little sister is dead when he sees her motionless body at the bottom of the steps. In his panic Ray believes for a second it is possible for him to turn this thing around. One of her arms is askew. The elbow is facing the wrong way. He sees her other arm, twisted behind her back and realizes that it is broken too. Two wrecked arms, at the very least. He looks back over his shoulder at the mother who speaks through a cloud of smoke.

"Is she okay, Ray? I...I didn't mean to push her so hard."

Ray is afraid to touch her in case he causes more damage where there is already far too much. "Call an ambulance, Mum. Hurry up!"

"An ambulance," she says. "Surely not."

"An ambulance, Mum. Right now!"

CHAPTER 17
The Present

Emma was a *Winnipeg Free Press* delivery person. Her job grew easier and more pleasant as summer approached. Some mornings were so clear and still that she wondered if they were real. Or if she was real in them. She often felt detached, disconnected from the life of the world. It was like looking at a picture in the art gallery and wishing she was in it. That happened sometimes. And it happened walking down Lyndale Drive on her paper route.

Why do I feel this way? she wondered. What's holding me back? From the outside looking in I would probably appear to be a part of this scene. But I don't feel it.

There were dog-walkers and exercise freaks in the early morning. She loved the dogs and some of the people weren't so bad. There was a fluffy white dog named Easy who was her favourite. He was some elaborate purebred and should have been a snob, but what did he know? So he leapt and squealed and received Emma's attentions just like the mongrels. The man who walked Easy was nice too. His name was Rupe. Emma liked sharing the mornings with these two.

Sometimes their cat came too. Emma envied them this. She wondered if she could teach her cat, Hugh, to follow along on her route. She doubted it.

It was after Easy and Rupe were out of sight that Emma noticed the long car with its closed windows creeping along behind her. It seemed out of place in the morning streets and normal people didn't drive that slowly. Except for Gus, and this was no Buick. It worried her.

She wished Easy would appear again around the next bend in the road. Or even the Marlboro Man, as Emma had come to call him. He smoked while he walked and Emma got a kick out of him. But the Marlboro Man didn't walk on Wednesdays.

She felt sure by now that the car was connected to her in some way. But she also worried that maybe she was just being paranoid. And she didn't want to embarrass herself with her own dark imagination. Time and again she found herself imagining the worst. Picturing death and pain and closed-up spaces. And her dad going out the door into the rain and never coming home. She saw herself by his grave at a policeman's funeral, where they would give her his badge or hat or whatever they presented the wife with. Because of course the wife wouldn't be there. Just Emma. And Sadie and Garth. And then she alone would be responsible for them. It would be just her.

She finished up the last of her papers and started to make a beeline for home. The car had disappeared but still she felt uneasy and resented the urgent feeling that pushed her home in such a hurry. What was the point of being up at this hour if you couldn't enjoy it?

Her wagon rattled along behind her till she turned into her own yard and abandoned it on the lawn.

"Hi, Mr. Olsen." She waved to Gus who was digging in his front garden.

"Howdy, Emma. Beautiful morning, eh?"

"Yeah, I guess so." She ran up the steps and into the house closing the door behind her against the cool spring air.

Nobody was up yet. This was the time that she usually spent reading her copy of the newspaper. But she didn't feel like it today. Just the deaths to see if Esme Jones' longer obituary had turned up yet. It hadn't.

Gus had been thinking about the Lincoln Town Car from the other night. He couldn't get it out of his head. He must make a point of speaking to Frank about it, although he realized what he had to say didn't amount to much. Maybe he was making a mountain out of a molehill.

Such a wisp of a girl, he thought, when Emma turned into her yard. Thirteen she was, but she looked like a child still, with her pale features and slight frame. He didn't doubt that she would blossom soon. It all happened so fast at that age. But she seemed slow physically and Gus figured that must be a relief for Frank. He could imagine the anguish of being the father of a beautiful daughter that first boys and then men couldn't wait to get their hands on. Poor Frank.

CHAPTER 18

Frank sat at his desk thinking about Jane Mallet. It was time to make a visit to the River City Health Centre. It had been called the River City Mental Hospital when Frank was a boy. And according to legend, it had started out as the River City Lunatic Asylum.

He drove a few miles south of the city to the grand old structure on the banks of the Red. It'd had its very own dike built after the flood of 1950. New wings had been added to the original building in the sixties and again in the eighties. Administration was still located in the old part. Frank knew this because his work as a policeman had brought him here before.

Frank loved old buildings. It was easy to pretend while he walked these halls that it was 1910 and he was sauntering toward the head nurse's office to talk with her in her starched whites about the criminal lunatics under her care. He could be smoking a cigarette or even a cigar. Like Emma.

The head psychiatric nurse was new. Her name was Norma Wayne and she didn't look anything like the nurse Frank had conjured up in his mind's eye.

She didn't try to hide her surprise when he inquired about a nurse named Jane Mallet.

"We don't have a nurse here by that name but we do have a patient." She pulled up Jane's file on her computer screen.

"She's been here a long time, our Jane."

"How long?"

Nurse Wayne gave Frank a flirtatious smile but didn't answer.

"Do you think I could have a copy of her file to take away with me?" Frank asked.

"Do you have a warrant?"

"No."

She laughed. "Well then, no, you may not."

"May I look at it while I'm here?"

"No. You may not."

"How about if you read it to me, Ms. Wayne?"

She laughed again. "That sounds like the most fun idea so far but I'm afraid I can't do that either. You know that, Inspector Foote."

"Frank. Please call me Frank."

"Okay, Frank. If you'll call me Norma."

Norma was willing to admit that there wasn't any record of the patient having been pregnant. "But that doesn't rule it out," she said. "More than once at my former place of employment a baby popped out unannounced. It wouldn't surprise me. No, it wouldn't surprise me a bit."

Nurse Norma Wayne sighed and smoothed her red skirt over her thighs. She sat up straight at a table that didn't really qualify as a desk in Frank's opinion. There were no drawers. Where would you hide your stuff?

I guess head nurses don't have to follow a dress code these days, he thought, as he took in the snugly fitting skirt and high heels. Far too high for a nurse. For any prairie person. They belonged in Bangkok.

"I'd be lying if I said we were able to keep an eye on all the patients all the time." Norma leaned back in her chair. "We quite simply can't. There aren't enough of us and it's getting worse."

Frank could tell exactly what her breasts would look like naked. Nicely shaped, medium sized and supple.

She caught him before he had a chance to determine if he was seeing her nipples or just a trick of the material in her silk shirt.

She smiled as she adjusted her reading glasses on her toy soldier nose. Her nose was the one thing about her that wasn't beautiful. It was a relief.

"Sometimes I think the old way, sterilizing patients, wasn't as barbaric as they make it sound," she said.

"It was a very small baby," Frank said. "It wouldn't have been hard to hide."

He didn't want to hear any more of Nurse Wayne's opinions. He'd rather think about her nose. It looked exactly like the cylindrical pieces of wood glued onto the faces in Garth's wooden soldier camp.

"Well, there you are, then." She snipped off the words. "One more very small unwanted baby in the world." She looked heavenwards, puffing a breath upwards so it lifted the fine hair of her bangs off her pretty forehead.

She smelled like licorice.

"I don't know the half of it?" Frank guessed.

"You said it, Frank. You don't know the half of it."

"Would you mind checking to see if there was any trouble with Jane Mallet last October? Or if she had any passes out of here for a day or a weekend or whatever around that time?"

Frank pressed on. He had established by now that Norma Wayne was a blabbermouth. She had to work very hard at not giving Frank the information he wanted.

"Fra-ank." She sang out his name. "You're pushing me-ee."

"Yes, Norma, I am." He smiled.

"Okay. This is the last question I'm going to answer." She fiddled on her keyboard. "Let's see. Jane doesn't get passes out of here. She could if there was someone to accompany her, but there isn't. She's a sad case, your Jane Mallet. She does go on excursions sometimes with a group from the hospital, swimming and whatnot. Those are fairly tightly supervised. Okay, October you say? No. No report of anything untoward."

"Was she sick around then at all? Did anyone come to visit her?"

"I don't know and I don't know," Nurse Wayne replied. "Look, Frank, I really can't tell you anything else, unless you get the necessary paperwork. I'm going to leave you here for a few minutes while I see to a matter on one of the wards." She winked. "I expect you to behave yourself while I'm gone."

A printer sat on the table next to the computer. Frank got it going and stuffed his briefcase with as many pages of Jane's life as he could before hearing Norma's cheery voice in the outer office. He stopped printing and turned off the machine. It clicked and sputtered to a halt as the doorknob turned and she swished into the room. She left the door ajar this time. The visit was over.

Frank settled himself in his car and pulled the pages out of his briefcase. He read what he had.

Mr. and Mrs. Mallet had been killed in a car crash on the August long weekend in 1969, on their way to a rock festival near Denver. A couple of weeks before Woodstock, Frank thought. Too bad they hadn't driven east instead of west.

The one-year-old girl, Jane, had been hurt but the file didn't go into the nature of her injuries. After a lengthy hospital stay she was placed in a foster home while she awaited readoption. It never happened. Frank guessed that must have been because of the nature of her injuries; she was, after all, in a mental hospital. She spent the next seventeen years being shifted from foster home to foster home with the occasional stay in an institution.

The piece of paper, the order of adoption from 1968 with her birth mother's name on it, must have followed along with her for a while, at least till she was old enough to read it and understand what it meant.

Grim, Frank thought. Very, very grim. Even without craziness bred in her bones or inflicted on her through injury, there was enough woe in the life of Jane Bower Mallet to turn her into a loon.

She had lived at River City for approximately nine years. She had admitted herself in the fall of '86 and been here ever since.

Frank's breath caught in his throat as he read on: In 1991 Jane Mallet had a complete hysterectomy after years of painful endometriosis.

So much for his hunch.

He found Jane in her room. She sat by a window gazing out at the big Manitoba sky. Frank wondered if it was the sky she saw or if she was looking at something else, a picture behind her eyes.

She turned around to look at him. She looked her age, twenty-seven, but there was something odd about her. Her skin was so smooth. There wasn't a line or a ripple, Frank realized, on a face untroubled by years of decision making and responsibility that form a part of a normal person's life. Her face was a blank.

Jane smiled like he was the only visitor she'd ever had. Her face lit up and Frank's heart ached for this woman who was so alone through no fault of her own.

"Hello, Jane," Frank said.

"Hello," she said. "Are you the police?"

"Why yes, I am," Frank said. "How did you know?"

"I know what you're here for," she said. "Are you going to arrest me?"

She talked slowly, haltingly, just as Greta had said, with lots of pauses.

"No, Jane dear, I certainly am not. Why would you think such a thing?"

"Because I lied," she said. "I lied to my real mother when I told her I was a nurse, when I told her I was married."

"Those are just tiny white lies, Jane. No one blames you for those. No. I just came to say hello really. I know your mother. She lives on my street. May I sit down a minute?"

Frank straddled a chair across from her and peered into her face. "Why did you write to your mother, Jane?" he asked. "Why did you phone her?"

"I dream about her. I dreamed her voice and I wanted to see if she really sounded that way, the way I dreamed."

"And did she?"

"I don't know."

"Would you like to see your mother, Jane?"

"I don't know." She cast her eyes down. "Why are you looking at me?"

"You look a bit like your mother," Frank said. "Just a bit."

Frank would tell Greta about Jane; he was certain she would want to know. But not today. He was suddenly very tired today.

CHAPTER 19

Denise spent the night in and out of sleep. When morning came she felt a queasiness in her stomach and achy all over but she'd had worse awakenings.

The curtains around her bed had been pushed back so when she sat up she could look both ways and see that all the other beds were occupied. Hers was in the middle, right across from the nursing station.

She had no idea how long she had been here.

Sun poured in the windows of the old building and landed on the two nurses at their station, some of it spilling over to one corner of Denise's bed.

"Good morning, Denise," the one named Ralph called.

An inkling of hope reared up and lay back down. Denise knew it was good that she woke up in this bed. She liked the small amount of routine that was provided for her here; she was good with routines.

It had occurred to her on occasion that she would have been a good candidate for the army, with all those early risings, physical training drills, shiny boots and punishments. Or the headmistress of a girls' school, or better yet, the assistant headmistress. If she was going to do something properly she wanted someone else to tell her what it was. I am an unenviable person, thought Denise.

The breakfast trays arrived and the smiling Ralph slid one onto her bedside table.

"Thanks." She swung her legs over the side of the bed a little too quickly and had to lie down again. She saw a stainless steel teapot on her tray and felt bile rise in her throat. Bracing herself on her elbows, she willed the vomit back down, tasting it.

"Ralph, wait. They've sent me tea. Is it possible for me to get coffee? I really hate tea, especially first thing in the morning."

Ralph no longer had a smile on his face. Maybe it hadn't been there in the first place.

"Mmm, not really," he said. "There should be some instant coffee in the lounge if you want to make some yourself."

Denise put on her robe and slippers and went through the double swinging doors into an empty hall.

In the washroom she splashed cool water on her face. Looking in the mirror, she was surprised and grateful that she didn't look worse. The skin around her eyes had a bruised look, but that had been there forever.

She stuck out her tongue at her reflection. Turned it upside down. Her one trick. That'd be sure to impress someone.

"You're going to die," she said. She leaned her forehead against the mirror. Her eyes hurt so badly she wanted to pluck them from their sockets and stomp on them. Burst and deflate them.

"I could be blind," she said. Blind would be better than this. No it wouldn't. Please, God, I didn't think that. Don't make me blind.

Denise vomited into the sink.

Why am I so wide awake all of a sudden? she wondered. They must have had me on something and taken me off it.

The last few days were a blur, images fighting for space at the front of her mind: a woman lying in her own filth, her own voice calling for a nurse. What day was it?

The lounge was empty but held the stale smoke of last night's insomniacs. She tried the small dirty window but it wouldn't budge. It looked out onto the parking lot of the emergency room where she had been admitted. Ambulance attendants were unloading someone while a small elderly woman watched. Probably her life mate of sixty years was on his way out and she didn't have a shoulder to lean on. Or, maybe it was a death long overdue and in her mind she was tripping the light fantastic.

The room contained two brown Naugahyde couches that looked eighty years old, and a few metal folding chairs. In the centre of the room was a low wooden table that held an assortment of old copies of *Field and Stream* and *Golf Digest*. The walls had been painted green many years before and the whole effect matched the way Denise felt on the inside. A perfect fit.

She found the kettle and a jar of instant coffee on a table in the corner. The coffee was decaf and the jar was empty.

Dr. Wim Winston walked into the lounge carrying two large coffees from Tim Horton's. For a moment, Denise wondered if she was hallucinating.

"Wim?"

"Hi, Denise."

He said her name the same, as though it was something that he wanted to have his way with. She remembered that it used to make her crazy to hear him say her name. It no longer had that effect on her.

"I saw that you had been admitted. I'm working in emergency now."

"Is one of those for me?"

He handed her one of the paper cups. "Black. Right?"

"Right."

Wim had become one of those men who combed thin strands of lubed-up hair up over his head to the wrong side. One of the strands had come free and hung like a dirty noodle down almost to his shoulder on the side where it belonged.

"I came to see you before but you were sleeping," he said.

"What day is it?"

"Thursday."

Denise wondered how she could have been with this man. She'd known him since way back before Frank. He had been built like her husband, tall and skinny. Both men had filled out over the years, Wim more so than Frank. Even his head had filled out, the way some men's do. Frank's head had stayed thin.

Denise had thought she loved him a long time ago when love was based on fewer things. He said he loved her too back then, but he had given her up without a word at about the same time he entered medical school. And Denise had met Frank.

Wim Winston ended up marrying a fellow doctor. They had kids and lived somewhere nice and Denise envied them.

But that didn't mean much. She envied pretty well everyone, even other drunks whose situations differed from hers, or didn't. Everyone's life looked better than hers.

She should never have had children. Often she didn't feel like a mother at all. She felt younger than Emma. And no good to anyone.

Denise was so tired of herself, of her thoughts and of the feelings that choked her and moved like clenched fists up and down her esophagus.

"Oh, Denise," Wim said now. His eyes searched hers and she looked away.

"You're so beautiful," he said.

"What! I am not! I'm a mess, Wim. A complete mess."

"I'm going to help you." He came closer than he should have as a doctor and smoothed the hair away from her face.

She backed into the coffee table. It pressed into the backs of her knees. His hair smelled greasy.

"Apparently I'm supposed to want to help myself," she said, thinking that doctors shouldn't have dirty hair.

"Do you?" Wim asked.

"Sometimes."

Denise edged around him and perched on the end of one of the couches. She took a sip of her coffee and set it down.

Wim sat down beside her and took both of her hands in his. He brushed his lips against her hair and she leapt up and moved toward the door. He followed her.

"What are you doing, Wim? This is insane." She looked into his strange familiar face. "You can't be doing this."

"Why not?" he said and tried to kiss her lips.

"I just barfed, for one thing."

Denise backed out the doorway and made her way back to the ward.

She was exhausted. His being here wasn't a good thing. She regretted having ever slept with him, even if it was a lifetime ago. Was that why he thought he could touch her in that way? How could he think that? She dreaded seeing him again, hoped he'd leave her alone.

Dread and regret. Regret and dread. Denise didn't own anything solid and true. She felt like one of those cartoon characters made up of broken lines, indicating ghostliness, invisibility.

Her head throbbed and her knees buckled as she tottered toward her bed. Ralph was stripping the sheets from the narrow mattress as she approached and there was nowhere for her to be.

Her last conscious thought as her legs crumpled beneath her was of her father leaning over her bed performing an operation on her with a familiar-smelling liquid. She was six and had gone to sleep with bubble gum in her mouth. It had fallen into her hair while she slept and this whole removal process started before she woke up. Her dad was gentle. Her mum was in the background giving the orders. Not gentle.

When Denise came to, she was in her newly made bed and Ralph was hovering.

She looked away. Her eyes burned and her lips felt caked with something. She didn't want to look at Ralph. He smelled medicinal. Or maybe that was her.

Denise didn't like Ralph. He didn't love her and she needed someone there who did, if there was such a person. Or else she wasn't going to be able to do this.

She drifted off again inside a dream about Garth. Her little boy.

She is sitting in a lawn chair with her feet resting on the edge of a plastic wading pool. It's so hot, the hottest day of the year and the whole family is in the yard cooling off in the sprinkler and pool. Garth fills his toy pail with water and pours it slowly over her feet. The cool water, the cool, cool water is better than a swim in the ocean. Garth is matter-of-fact about his action; he isn't smiling. His pink tongue sticks conscientiously out the side of his mouth. He's helping. Her Garth.

Ray sits as far away from her as he can in the back seat of the '53 Ford. They're in trouble. They were arguing over which station to listen to on the car radio and the mother turned it off. Ray wants CKY with Del Shannon singing "Runaway." She wants CKRC with Connie Francis singing "Where the Boys Are." The mother wants them to shut up. They do.

They're on the highway between Starbuck and Fannystelle. It's as dark as night gets in the summer on the prairies with the full moon and the stars and the odd lamp-lit farmhouse. The kids were rousted from their beds to satisfy the whim of their mother. She thinks it's the right time to introduce her newest friend, Cy, to her relatives in Morden. It's Cy's car; he lets their mother drive while he leans against the passenger door in the front seat. He snores and she pokes him from time to time. Cy snorts awake and mutters some, then settles back into a regular rhythm.

"Stop!" Ray yells. "Mum, stop!" The mother didn't see the awkward angle of the headlights shining out of the ditch or if she did, chose to keep on driving. But her son's shouts make her slam on the brakes and bring the car to a screeching halt before she has a chance to think. The four of them hurtle forwards and then sideways as she jerks the old Ford onto the soft shoulder.

Ray leaps out of the car before it has stopped moving. "It's an accid-" he cries.

Those are the last words he speaks, before the semi-trailer clips him and the car door from their places on the road and catapults them into the starry night. She runs after her brother. No one tries to stop her. She finds him, without his glasses, staring up at her from his bed of flax. She kneels to hold him, to give him some of what he has so often given her. But she sees there is no one there to hold. It's just a face, on its own, flat on the blue night field of flax.

She hears the voice of Connie Francis coming from the car radio. She thinks that if someone changed the station, if she could hear Del Shannon's familiar voice singing "Runaway," she would have her brother back, intact. He would be more than a face in the flax.

CHAPTER 21
The Present

In a room in a house with windows facing the swollen Assiniboine River, Simon Grace lay on a couch worrying about Ivy. He was afraid he had made a mistake in marrying her. The thought made him laugh out loud. They had been together for nearly twenty years.

Simon lay under a quilt with pillows propping him up so he could watch the river. He was seventy-seven years old and not feeling very well. He had hoped for comfort in his old age and knew that he wasn't going to get it, except for what he could manage to provide for himself.

It had started out perfectly. Ivy had wanted to please him and she had. She knew how to look and exactly what to say, sometimes to a fault. He found himself wanting to see a hair out of place, wanting to see her drunk, letting something slip.

He never knew her at all, even in the beginning, he realized now. Oh, they had golfed and dined and traveled together. They had even talked and kissed and laughed together. But she was always like a date for him, on her best behaviour. He had never heard her hiccup. And she left the room if she felt a sneeze coming on.

She had done her duty by him, he supposed, if duty was what you were looking for, in exchange for the security he had to offer. He never kidded himself that it had been anything more than that. But he couldn't keep himself from expecting more.

Everyone warned him against her: his kids, his friends, his colleagues, even his ex-wife, Irene, who he knows did it from a good place in her heart. Oh, she was jealous, of course she was. How could she, at fifty-five, have competed with Ivy in her early twenties? She didn't even try, just packed her bags. And then spurned his offer of the house because that was where she had found them together.

Ivy had engineered that, he was sure of it. The house on Wellington Crescent was a necessary part of the package. The Simon Grace package.

He thought about Irene now and remembered how they used to swim together after dark up at the lake. Even later when the girls were all grown up. They'd pad down to the beach in their bathrobes and beach shoes and leave them by the water's edge. Their bodies had felt so good together in the cool water of Lake Winnipeg.

When he thought of Irene he always pictured her at Victoria Beach. That was where she loved it most. It was right that she have the cottage. He missed her and envied her too, with her connection to both girls. They hadn't come to see him for years. He had never seen his grandchildren. Maybe they didn't even know he existed.

He had paid heavily for choosing Ivy. But he had gone in with his eyes open. And now he didn't have enough strength left to try and get out.

But he would love to see his daughters; he had thought they'd come round.

With all Ivy's attributes, her skills at running his household, acting as hostess, volunteering at the museum, and without question appearing beautiful on his arm, she couldn't manage any warmth. Simon saw her try. She tried so hard it hurt him to watch. But she couldn't do it. And he could live with that. With the coolness.

But something had changed in the last few years. There was something else now. She had purpose for the first time since he had known her, a purpose that he was sure wasn't connected to him. And he feared it, sensed that it didn't bode well. It was practically a living thing, dwelling in the house with them, moving through the rooms like a poison mist.

It had started a couple of years back and intensified during the year that she spent away. A year and some months ago, Ivy went to Vancouver for a while. She told him she wanted to take some computer courses at an expensive west coast school, better herself.

Ivy hadn't been in the work force for years—since he'd married her, in fact. Why would she need to sharpen her computer skills?

"You don't need bettering," he had said.

"You know I do," she said and bared her teeth. A smile.

When Ivy returned she said nothing about her courses and Simon didn't ask. He wasn't sure he wanted to know what she'd been up to. He had no idea how she had spent her time in Vancouver. She had looked so beautiful when she came back last fall. Whatever she'd done agreed with her. She had glowed. She'd filled out in a way that appealed to Simon. And her clothes were different, long and flowing. They suited her new softness.

Simon thought that women today, including Ivy, were far too concerned about staying overly slim. He'd loved her new look, but he wasn't allowed to touch. That had stopped a long time ago.

But anyway, Ivy's plumpness was short-lived. She had worked very hard at slimming down again, and toning up, exercising like a fiend.

Simon started to cry now, a few thin tears at first and then his body was wracked with sobs. His loneliness suffused him like a drug, entering every vein, every cell.

"It's too late," he moaned, surprising himself with his words. "It's too late," he said again before fear clutched his insides when he saw Ivy looking in through the window at him. She had come around the back way. Who knew why? Who knew why this woman did anything? But it was too late. She had seen him crying and perhaps had even heard him. He cringed with embarrassment.

Ivy chose not to come in, but walked back around the front of the house to another entrance. He was grateful for that, grateful for her aversion to him in his mire of loneliness.

His hand fell down to touch the head of Lucy, the black lab that had kept him company for the last thirteen years. She snuffled contentedly in her sleep. She wasn't feeling very well these days either and Simon knew he was going to have to put her down soon. He would like to die along with her. If only it were that easy.

"Oh, Lucy girl, we're a fine old pair."

He scratched her gently behind her ear. He wanted her to wake up. She stirred and licked his hand before settling her head between her paws to continue her snooze. Simon sighed and closed his eyes.

He could hear Ivy moving in another part of the house. It sounded as if she was in his study. What possible reason could she have for being there, for carrying her poison into his private sanctuary? He knew he wouldn't mention it to her. He feared her. It wasn't a specific fear, like a fear of dying or a fear of high places. It was vaguer than that: a fear that she could cause harm in ways he wasn't even able to imagine.

"My wife scares the hell out of me, Lucy."

The dog slept on and Simon lay stiff under his quilt and stared straight up at the ceiling.

Ivy ran her fingers along the smooth edge of the flawless oak desk. She liked the feel of the wood, well-cared for over decades of use. And she liked the smell of this room too. It was leather and paper and the lemon oil that Lena used to polish up the old wood.

Simon's computer sat on the desk. After months of trying, with no success, Ivy's prayers had led her here. She had realized that the Internet could be a useful tool for her. She used it to find information that helped her in the execution of her plan. It led her to the decision to spend one year away from home, in Vancouver. If she couldn't accomplish it in a year, then she would…well, she hadn't known what she would do next.

Now she'd been back from the coast for several months and was biding her time. She still prayed every day at mid-morning, but Gruck was seldom there to answer her. Sometimes another voice came. Male. This voice confused her because it was soothing and led her in comfortable directions. It interfered with the plans G had for her. And so did the Squeaks, though she could never remember her Squeak-related thoughts.

The last thing G had told her was to contact Frank Foote, but Ivy felt she needed more. She couldn't go to visit Frank and have absolutely nothing to say, could she? She was starting to think that she might have to trust that Gruck would advise her after she got there.

If the influence of the male voice and the Squeaks continued to erode her plan, it would mean the last two years, four months, five days, sixteen hours and—she looked at her watch—five minutes, would have been for nothing and that made her head scream.

She would have to go ahead. If G didn't show up in the room with her the worst that would happen is that she would make a fool of herself. She could do that.

Ivy stared at her surroundings. She envied the people who were lucky enough to really belong in such a room. She knew it was hers; that had been the plan. But she still felt as though she was outside with her dirty face pressed against the window of the room with the blazing fire and the family photos on the grand piano. Not her family.

She pulled the chain on the desk lamp and it made little difference in the late afternoon light. She pulled it again. And again. Again. Then she counted the items on the desk and made a note of the number on a slip of paper that she took from its hiding place behind *Fifth Business*. Robertson Davies was her husband's favourite writer and he owned all his books. They were lined up in order in the middle of a shelf directly across the room from his desk. So he could see them and admire them, she supposed. A few of the books were signed by the author himself and her husband loved that fact.

She pulled *The Rebel Angels* from its place on the shelf and moved it one over, to the other side of *What's Bred in the Bone*. Then she smiled. That'd throw him for a loop. She left the room and closed the door behind her.

Lena watched her leave and Ivy saw her but pretended that she didn't. She didn't feel like having to think of any words to say to the housekeeper or cook or nurse or whatever she was. Ivy could feel her hatred. This was what Dr. Braun had called paranoia and Ivy had tried for a while to think of hatred differently. But it was too hard. She had quit Dr. Braun and his needling ways. It was close to three years now since her last visit to his downtown office.

She had gone to see him once a month for several years, at Simon's insistence. He had been worried about her nightmares, her screams in the night. Mostly the doctor just prescribed drugs, but now and then toward the end he had wanted her to talk and that was why she had quit.

She didn't want to talk, not in the sense that he wanted her to. Why talk? It hurt—like her nightmares. And the drugs pretty much took care of those.

That was the only bad part about not going to see him anymore. Without him there were no pills. She knew she screamed again at night sometimes because she woke herself up with it. But she was pretty sure it was only now and then.

She had almost decided to go back to Dr. Braun, to make up things to talk about that wouldn't hurt. So she could get the pills back. But then her plan had been set in motion. And her plan was almost as good as the drugs for stopping her nightmares.

She slept at the other end of the house from Simon now so when she did scream it probably didn't bother him as much as it used to when they had shared a bed. One night she had frightened him so badly he thought he was having a heart attack. They actually ended up chuckling about it in the brightness of the next morning. But in the heart of that dark night there had been no laughter.

Ivy considered visiting her husband on his couch now. But she shuddered at the thought of his sniveling old form under the quilt. She snatched up her car keys from the hall table and headed out the front door with no particular destination in mind. Just away from here.

CHAPTER 22

Emma and Delia went for a walk after supper. They didn't have much homework these days with school being almost over. And they'd had two substitute teachers today. One in science and one in geography.

"Do you think Miss Forbes is away because we're driving her insane?" Emma asked.

"Maybe."

"I think she was actually crying yesterday." Emma wore a huge sweater that slipped down to expose one pale thin shoulder and she kept trying to push it back up where she felt it belonged.

"I hate this stupid top," she said.

"Don't worry about it." It was Delia who had talked her into the sweater in the first place. "It looks cool when it's falling off."

She reached over and plucked it off Emma's shoulder so it fell back to where she thought it should be.

"Anyway," Emma said, "I thought maybe we should ease up on her a bit when she comes back."

"Who?"

"Miss Forbes. I mean with the humming and everything."

Delia wasn't listening. Donald and another boy from their homeroom, Richard, skidded to a halt beside them at the curb.

"Hi."

"Hi."

"What's up with you?" Richard asked.

"Nothin' much," Delia said. "Just hangin' around."

Donald stared at Emma and Emma stared back.

"We were just talking about Miss Forbes," she said, "thinking maybe we should be nicer to her when she comes back. I think we might be driving her crazy. Like, literally."

"I think you might be right," Donald said. "Especially with the humming. She can't tell where it's coming from when a lot of us are doing it and she doesn't know who to yell at."

"Yeah, it's kind of pitiful," Emma said.

Donald reached over from his bike and gently placed Emma's sweater up on her shoulder where she thought it belonged. Her inclination was to turn her eyes away. But she held his gaze, feeling herself enter delicious new territory. Delicious and very scary.

"See ya."

"See ya."

The boys sped away and Emma could feel Donald's fingers on her skin. She lowered herself to the curb and sat with both arms hugging her mid-section. Her stomach did crazy things.

"Delia, he touched me," she said. "I'm gonna marry him. Did you see what he did? He did do it, didn't he? Did you see it, what he did?"

"He loves you, Em." Delia smiled. "Let's go get cigars and like, celebrate."

CHAPTER 23

The trail leading away from Greta Bower's rain barrel was ice cold. Detective Sergeant Fred Staples had checked with hospitals in the two neighbouring provinces and come up with nothing. They were officially out of ideas.

All Frank had was a feeling that came and went, that it had everything to do with at least one of Greta's stepbrothers, Dwight or Duane Simkins. But Duane was in jail and Dwight was dead. So how could that be?

Frank checked with the prison system in Quebec and confirmed Duane's incarceration. He had killed an off-duty policewoman so he wouldn't be released in the foreseeable future. Frank checked further and found out that Dwight had been killed during the commission of the same crime that sent his brother to jail. He was shot through the eye by an errant bullet from the gun of a third member of their bumbling gang.

Little Jane Doe's blood was in the fridge and there it would stay till they had something to compare it to.

Late Friday afternoon there was a knock on Frank's office door. He sighed and stuffed his knitting into a drawer. It had turned into a scarf for Emma, a good long one to keep her warm in winter. There really had been no decision to make about what the object would be. Who was he kidding? Scarves were all he knew how to do.

"Come in, Fred."

Fred had wanted to come by and talk about the case. He didn't like unsolved mysteries. Frank was thinking that sometimes puzzles were better left unsolved. And further, that some were meant only to be known by Those Who Can't Be Seen. The same Ones Who Knew how many orgasms Frank had had in his life and how many times he had laughed.

Fred was very quiet for someone who wanted to talk. He didn't seem his usual soldierly self and there were dark circles under his eyes. They looked out of place on his tidy face.

"Are you all right, Fred?" Frank asked. "You don't seem yourself."

"Yes, sir. I'm fine. I just haven't been sleeping very well lately is all."

"Lots on your mind, eh?"

"I guess so, sir. I'd rather not talk about it if you don't mind."

"Of course. I'm sorry, Fred. I didn't mean to pry."

"No, it's okay. You weren't prying, sir."

Frank looked down at the thin file on his desk. The Rain Barrel Baby.

"It had to have been the mother who left her there," he said, veering away from the subject of young Fred's troubles. "Who else, except maybe some sort of slippery boyfriend?"

"I don't know, sir."

"One thing seems clear to me," Frank continued, "and that is that the mother was complicit in this crime. If she wasn't, then surely she would have reported a missing baby. Wouldn't she?"

"I guess so, sir."

"It's impossible to guess people's motives these days," Frank said. "It seems harder than it used to be. Maybe I'm getting stupider, or maybe people's reasons for doing things really are getting more complicated."

"You're not getting stupider, sir."

Frank smiled at his sergeant and wondered why he had come. "Is there anything in particular you want to discuss, Fred?" He glanced toward his wool drawer.

"I guess not, sir. I just thought maybe we could bounce ideas back and forth till we came up with something."

Frank chuckled. "I'm afraid I've about bounced everything I have, Fred. Right now anyway. Is there anything you'd like to add?"

"I guess not."

"Well, in that case, I'm going home. And on the way I'm going to stop at Greta Bower's house to tell her that we're not closing the case, but that we're no longer going to actively pursue it. I'm pretty sure she won't care, but we should keep her posted."

"Goodnight then, sir."

"Goodnight, Fred. Take it easy."

Frank wanted to ask him again not to call him "sir," but didn't think now was the time. Fred had something on his mind and Frank worried about him in spite of his effort not to.

He decided to wait till after supper and then till after Garth and Sadie were in bed before walking down the back lane to speak to Greta. He would tell her, too, about his Wednesday afternoon visit with Jane. She could do what she pleased with the information.

The sun was just setting and lights were going on in the houses. As Frank reached for her gate he saw Greta through the sliding glass doors to her dining room. She was naked and she was rubbing something onto her skin. He watched, motionless, as she massaged the lotion into her breasts with particular gentle care.

Frank knew he couldn't go in to see her but he also couldn't walk away.

This woman is wacko, Frank thought. What if I were a rapist or a murderer? Or a Peeping Tom? He watched the motion of her hands on her body for a few more moments and then forced himself to turn around and trudge back down the lane.

A great sadness entered Frank as he sorted laundry in the basement of his house. He threw in a load and went upstairs to kiss his kids goodnight.

And as for letting Greta know the status of the rain barrel case, he would call Fred in the morning and ask him to drop by on her. He should have done that in the first place.

He'd have to tell her about Jane himself, though. He couldn't pawn that one off on his sergeant.

But not tonight. Maybe even not tomorrow. But soon.

CHAPTER 24

Ivy had lived out the entire year away from the big house on Wellington Crescent because her prayers hadn't told her to go back. She had what she needed after five months, but had stayed in Vancouver because Gruck had told her: one year.

Now as she lay in the big brass bed that she shared with no one she recalled the Saturday night her search had ended. She had wanted to die before he stopped. She had wanted him to nail her to the wall. He had hurt her almost enough.

He was also the one. She knew it as surely as if it had been emblazoned on his forehead.

"You've got AIDS, don't you?" she asked.

"I don't know. Possibly," he said. "Probably, I guess."

"Why did you have sex with me then?"

Ivy knew she must be sad because she felt a tear make its way down the soft curve of her cheek. It had been a long time since she had cried.

"Why do you fuck people when you know you may be killing them?" she asked.

"Because I don't care." He stroked himself and grew hard again.

"You don't fuck like you don't care." Ivy touched his hand, the one that held his dick.

He shook her off.

"I care about fucking," he said. "Just not about you."

The words stung, like pain from another life, one already lived. She was going to use his gift of death, she had shopped for it. But still, the toxic dart of his uncaring clouded her vision for a few seconds. She brushed the tear aside, there was just the one.

"Would you mind once more?" she asked when her voice returned. "A rear entry this time?"

She had made little nicks in herself with a razor blade, front and back, before going out to find a man. She always did that. It didn't hurt to help things along. And she took a form of pleasure, too, in the pain the nicks provided. One of the few pleasures she could manage.

Afterwards, the man made Ivy wait till he was ready to come again. This time on her face. No touching, no movement.

No problem.

He hadn't even taken his boots off.

After he left, Ivy lay on the bed and stared at the ceiling. There was no space in her life for words that could hurt her, so she buried them. Deep. Like nuclear waste in salt rooms under the ocean. No leaking in this lifetime.

Phase One of her plan was complete and she knew that this was where the hard part began. It had been easy to get any old guy to fuck her. What came next was entirely different. Her work was cut out for her. Ivy had received inklings of what came next, but no particulars.

On the Sunday morning after the Saturday night that she met with success Ivy lingered in the park across the street from a cathedral. It was too damp to sit. Fog bathed Vancouver but the sun was there in the sky beyond. She could see it.

"I've done it," she said. "I have what I need." She realized she had spoken aloud and laughed. It didn't matter. What mattered was the damp grass and the open doors of the cathedral and the sun beyond the mist. She watched the church people come and go.

My God, what have I done? The realization of what she had achieved struck a blow to her chest that brought her to her knees in the wet grass of the church park.

She had been to a clinic and it had been confirmed. She was HIV-positive. It was underway.

Seven months later, on her way home, Ivy was slightly breathless and her chest felt heavy underneath her traveling clothes.

She was pregnant. For the second time in her life. The first time, she had wanted the baby. But he had been taken from her. She hadn't even held him, didn't know where he had gone. She often pictured him at the river, cold and alone.

This time she didn't want the baby. It was a death child. And it had made her fat, just when she needed most to be perfect. It was an unexpected and unfortunate complication, but Ivy had decided to incorporate it into her plans. What else could she do with it?

She would return to the house on Wellington Crescent and wait for her time to come. It wouldn't be long now; she could feel it getting ready inside her. Simon need never know. She wondered if she could pull that off and knew that she could. This was not a big baby, not a big deal.

And then she would…well, she hadn't quite figured that part out yet. But she would do something marvelous with it. She would punish somebody with this baby.

And then she would wait and listen for the next step. And after everything, when it was finally over, she could die alongside Simon. A warm feeling settled in her chest, crept into the empty spaces surrounding the weight. She almost looked forward to seeing her husband, her protector, the only one she'd had since Ray.

She smelled apple blossoms mixed with the painfully sweet scent of the plum. She heard a radio playing softly, a song from 1961. There was a tender movement at the very corner of her consciousness. For just a moment she felt that everything was going to be all right.

But the warm feeling didn't last. She had closed her eyes then and waited for sleep.

Ivy felt hollow now as she swung her long legs over the side of the bed. It was time to get started on the day, such as it was. It hadn't occurred to her that Gruck wouldn't always be there to guide her. Her only comfort was that death was hers already. She wouldn't have to plod on and on, through brittle middle-age to a bleak and airless existence as a dry old crone. She'd be better off ashes, like her dad, like Ray.

Today she would go to see Frank Foote. It was Tuesday and Tuesdays were good. By herself she would take this next step. Maybe G was testing her to see if she had any ideas of her own. Well, she would try. She couldn't wait forever. Forever might not be that far away.

The male voice, the one she had come to call Reuben, came to her now and she leaned into it. It hinted at another plan and Ivy sighed with exhaustion. The task at hand was huge. She didn't want any more to do, but she supposed that she had no choice.

CHAPTER 25

"Psst! Happy birthday, Dad!" Emma caught Frank early, in the garage as he got into the car.

She had bought him a pile of wool in all different colours. She knew he wanted his knitting to be a secret, but she figured this would be okay. Besides, she couldn't pass it up. It had been displayed in an apple barrel outside the door of a going-out-of-business crafts store. Pink and deep blue and green and gold. Red and purple and orange and white. Some of the balls were even two-toned. Emma had wanted to dive into the barrel of wool. But she bought it instead, in its entirety. It cost quite a bit, even marked down the way it was. But she didn't care. She loved her dad and besides, her stupid mum probably wouldn't even remember his birthday, let alone buy him anything.

Emma had decided to give her dad the wool when no one else was around. That way she wouldn't be letting the cat out of the bag about his hobby. She understood how he might feel kind of funny about it. She knew she wouldn't want Donald or Vince or even Delia to see her dad knitting. They would make fun of him for sure.

The wool wasn't wrapped, just heaped mumbo jumbo into a plastic laundry basket with a big bow on top. The early sun shone through the small window high up on the garage wall, illuminating Emma and the basket of wool.

Her worry that he would be upset vanished when she saw the look on his face.

"Oh, Emmy. How did you know? Never mind. This is the most beautiful sight I've ever seen. You and a pile of wool, standing in a sunbeam."

He hugged her and blinked furiously to keep the tears from landing on her head. "Thank you, Em. This is the best birthday present I've ever had. Far and away the best."

CHAPTER 26
1963

The hardest thing about the other kids being so mean to her is the part when she goes home afterwards and her mother gives her that look. The one that says: You're pathetic. Useless. Can't you stand up to these bullies? Some of them aren't much bigger than you for Christ's sake!

She doesn't cry anymore. It is the only thing she can fight back with. No tears. The tall bony one doesn't like that. He pushes her some to get the results that his name calling can't.

Ivy's go-ot cooties! Ivy's go-ot cooties!

Her eyes stay dry and not a sound escapes her throat as she lies face down on the dirt of the baseball diamond.

She knows she can hang on. For what, she's not sure, but there must be something for her somewhere.

Her knees sting. There are pebbles in her wounds. They pushed her down this time and pulled her hair. Her shorts are ripped. She can't bear to think about the next time.

Ivy's dad's in he-ell! Ivy's dad's in he-ell!

Ivy lies with her face in the dirt till darkness enfolds her. No one comes. Her knees hurt but nothing is ruined. The sound of her own breath comforts her.

Why did he say that about her dad? Ivy never knew her dad. He died before she was born.

Ivy's dad's in hell, he said. Someone told him to shut up, to leave her dad out of it.

Ivy rises to her knees, then to her feet, and walks slowly across the baseball park. She passes the United Church with its tall pointed steeple. If only there was someone to hang around with, someone to be her friend. Then maybe they would leave her alone. But no one wants to be friends with her. What is it about her?

There is no one to tell. Telling her mother doesn't work. It just makes it worse. Her mother has her solitaire to play and her gin to drink.

And Wilf doesn't want to know. He is so old he's not like a brother at all. She misses Ray so much her whole body aches. She wishes it could have been her that died. Or both of them. That would be the best of all.

She counts the stars that begin to show themselves in the night sky. She thinks she has them all and then discovers another patch winking at her from the south and then from directly over her head. Spinning in circles in the middle of the schoolyard she tries to keep up with the stars. She can't, of course, and that's when the tears finally come.

At home she asks her mum why anyone would say that about her dad, that he was in hell.

"He's not in hell," says her mum. "That's a rotten thing to say. Those kids don't know nothin'. Your dad was sick, was what he was."

"Sick how?"

"He had spells."

"What do you mean? What kind of spells?"

"Just spells, okay? Leave me alone, Ivy."

Ivy soaps up a face cloth and gently washes her knees and applies iodine. She crawls into bed and finds a place at the back of one of Ray's old scribblers to try and write away her confusion and her hurt—to try and make sense of it.

There was a new boy tonight. He hung back though, didn't even pretend to want to join in. He was the one who told the bony guy to shut up about her dad. She knows she should be grateful for this, but she isn't. What difference does it make?

CHAPTER 27
The Present

Ivy walked toward the police station where Frank Foote worked.

The names and faces of the boys were hotly branded into the folds of her memory. She could manage not to think about them sometimes. Whole years had gone by without her giving them a thought.

When she first left home, she poured all her energies into staying alive. She had enlisted Wilf's help, the brother who wasn't Ray. The brother who wasn't dead. He paid two months' rent for her on a furnished room on Spence Street with a bathroom down the hall. It had seemed like heaven to Ivy—a place of her own. She wasn't quite sixteen, so she lied about her age. The lie came easily.

She found a waitressing job for the summer at the Salisbury House on West Broadway.

In the fall Wilf paid for a secretarial course at Success Commercial College. He knew it was a good investment. Ivy never let anyone down.

This was a good period in Ivy's life. She worked part time at the restaurant and learned how to type fifty-five words a minute.

She worked on herself as well: her physical appearance, the way she presented herself, even the way she talked. Her smooth hair, her flawless makeup, a blouse that was never untucked—these things helped her squash down the past, the place she had come from. She worked hard at pushing the images back. Back and back.

She imagined a different background for herself, one that was more acceptable—with a father and even a sister that she confided in. When she pictured the dad he always looked like Robert Young on *Father Knows Best*. Perfect. The sister was Patty Duke.

She didn't have to be the old Ivy anymore. She could be a brand new one who could do or think anything. And best of all, not think at all about certain things. Like her mother. And the boys.

She thought of the boys now, though, saw them in her mind's eye: Duane Simkin, black-hearted Duane; Dwight Simkin, his smelly brother; fat Ronnie Fowler; and Wim Winston.

And then, separate from the rest in a little picture frame all his own: Frank Foote.

Detective Sergeant Staples knocked on Frank's office door and stuck his head in.

"There's someone here to see you, sir."

Frank stuffed hanks of wool inside his middle drawer.

"Who is it? I was just thinking of leaving for lunch. Can't someone else see this person?"

He wanted to tell Fred about the gift his daughter gave him, but didn't suppose he would.

"She asked for you in particular."

"Who? Who is it, Fred?" Frank saw him noticing the wool.

"I don't know. She wouldn't tell me her name but she seems very nice."

"Good grief. Okay, tell her to come in, but I've only got a minute or two."

"Right, sir."

"Fred?"

"Yes, sir?"

"Could you please try and not call me 'sir'?"

"I'll try, Sss. Sorry. It's hard for me for some reason. I didn't forget that you asked me before. It's just that I find it so damn hard. But I'll try."

Fred looked troubled and Frank regretted having spoken.

"Don't worry, Fred. It's not important. Send in whoever the heck it is wants to see me and only me."

"You bet, Fffrank."

"All right, Fred!"

She smelled edible as she breezed into his office. It brought to mind cakes and summer kitchens. And he was glad now that he had taken the time to see this striking woman.

"What can I do for you?" he asked.

"Hello, Frank." She held out her gloved hand and he took it. Soft gloves, hard grip.

"Ivy. Ivy Grace," she said.

"How do you do?"

"You don't remember me, then." She spoke in a low voice, carefully modulated. It sounded worked on, trained.

Frank didn't have a clue. He peered at her closely, the thick dark hair, the expressionless face and the length of her, hidden inside a long camel coat. He looked back to her eyes but he had never seen such eyes. No clues there.

"No. I'm sorry." He had a feeling now that something big was happening. Big and bad. But he had no idea what.

"I used to be Ivy Srutwa." She laughed, just a heh! in her throat.

"Still am, I guess," she said, "though I've spent a long time trying to forget it."

Frank's scalp prickled.

"Ivy. Good God, yes! I remember you. Of course I do. It's just, well…you look so different. Great, mind you! Different and great."

Heartiness was all Frank could manage. A sick feeling welled up inside of him at the thought of Ivy Srutwa. At the picture of her lying in the penalty box with the stringy mess of the boys clinging to her face and hair.

"It's okay, Frank. Don't look so stricken. I remember, you know. I remember that you were the nice one. It's not the type of thing you forget."

"Ivy, I…"

"Frank, don't talk. Let me tell you why I'm here."

Frank was raising a stink, literally. He hoped he was far enough away from her that she wouldn't notice the smell of fear coming from his body and clothes. It happened in a second, along with the perspiration pouring down his face.

He fumbled in his pocket for the cotton handkerchief that had once belonged to his father. His mum had given it to him along with several others during the confusing week following his dad's death. She had thrown shoes and pipes and other useless things his way, but the handkerchiefs he had kept. They had been stained and crumpled but Denise had spruced them up for him and it usually gave him pleasure to take one from his pocket instead of a Kleenex. But not now.

It's odd, thought Frank, through the sweat of his panic, this woman must be almost as old as me. But she doesn't have any of the usual stuff that a face gets after all those years of living. No laugh lines, no frown lines, no worry lines. Like Jane Mallet.

But Frank knew that this was a surgical smoothness. She was beautiful, no doubt about that, but it was an unreal beauty, like those Elizabeth Taylor perfume ads. Frank felt doomed.

"Please sit down, Ivy. Forgive me. Why are you here?"

A feeling nudged at information buried deep in Frank's brain. An image of the rain barrel baby flashed behind his eyes.

She didn't sit but walked slowly to the window. Frank circled round the desk, staying as far from her as he could. When she turned back to him anyone looking at the scene would have thought it was her office and he was the nervous visitor. Even with her coat and gloves. And hat. Good God, she was wearing a hat! He hadn't noticed it at first. Her hair was black and so was the hat, but it was there all right, perched on the back of her head, a small pillbox, of the type women wore in the sixties when they wanted to be Jackie Kennedy.

"I want to ask a favour," she said.

A chill ran up Frank's back and mingled with the sweat.

"Okay. Is it a…uh…police matter?" he asked.

And waited for an answer.

He remembered that he had lent one of his dad's handkerchiefs to Greta Bower and he hoped that she would return it to him without his having to ask.

CHAPTER 28

"Dad, can we get a dog?"

Emma sat at the kitchen table with Frank and Gus. She had invited Gus for lunch as a surprise for her dad's birthday. Not much of a surprise really; they saw Gus pretty much every day. But it pleased both men and they ate enthusiastically. They had Emma's specialty: asparagus wrapped in bread, held together with toothpicks, then grilled and covered with hot mushroom soup. It was "Hot-dog Day" at Garth and Sadie's school and neither of them liked asparagus, so it worked out great.

They were finishing off with cocoa, complete with marshmallows on top.

"Oh, I don't think so, Emma," Frank said. "A dog is quite a bit of work, you know."

"I was thinking of a Labrador puppy. I've never met a Lab that wasn't extra specially nice. I'd train him and take him for walks and give him baths and feed him and do all the stuff that has to be done. I'd take him to the vet and pick up after him and teach him tricks."

"What about Hugh?" Frank reached over to where the cat lay upside down in Gus' arms and stroked his soft little belly. "He's a pretty good pet, isn't he?"

"Well, yeah. He's great. I love Hugh. I was just thinking how nice it would be to have a dog too. And it would be company for Hugh when no one's home."

"Oh, Emma." Frank sighed and looked at Gus, who busied himself neutrally with Hugh's ears.

"I can't walk Hugh." Emma began stacking their dirty dishes by the sink. Not a speck of food was left on anyone's plate.

"Great lunch, Emma. Thank you," Gus said.

"Yeah, thanks, Em. It was a real treat." Frank drank the last of his cocoa. "That oughta do me till supper."

"You're welcome. It was good, wasn't it?"

Emma remembered the sinister car from the other morning and thought how much better she would feel if she had a good dog bounding along beside her.

"A dog would be able to go places with me, accompany me," she said.

"You could try walking Hugh," Frank suggested. "He might let you."

Gus laughed. "I wouldn't bet on it. Not this little rascal." He winked at Emma.

"I saw that, Gus," Frank said. "Don't you two go ganging up on me now." He pushed out his chair and took his empty mug to the sink. "I mean it."

"It would be protection for me on my paper route."

Frank turned to face his daughter. "Has someone been bothering you, Em?"

"No."

"Are you sure? You'd tell me, wouldn't you?"

"Yeah."

"Promise me, now."

"There's nothing, Dad. Really."

Nothing I wouldn't feel stupid telling about anyway, Emma thought. There was a car on the street and it moved slowly. Yeah, and? That's it. End of story.

"Promise me you'll tell me if anything ever scares you on your route or anywhere else, Emma."

"I promise! Jeez."

"Okay. Now this dog business. I'm not saying no. I'm just saying, can we leave it for a bit? Like till things get straightened away with your mum and work settles down a little. I've got a couple of kind of troublesome cases on the go right now."

Emma muttered something.

"Pardon?" Frank asked.

"Things are never gonna be straightened away with Denise."

"Since when do you call your mother Denise?"

"Since right now, I guess. I don't know."

I shouldn't have asked him on his birthday, Emma thought, on her way back to school. It was tricky of me even though I didn't plan it and didn't mean it to be. I wanted lunch to be perfect and I ruined it by giving him another worry.

CHAPTER 29

Denise lay on top of her taut hospital sheets and daydreamed about her young self with Frank. Daydreamed about her own husband. One hot Winnipeg summer she had rented an apartment above a grocery store in the posh part of town. It was her first summer with Frank.

She was waiting tables and Frank was already a cop. They were crazy about each other. Wim had come around at that time and tried to get her to go with him again. Maybe he was even married by then. Denise closed her eyes against the memory of herself pushing Wim so hard out the door that he fell down the first flight of stairs to the second-storey landing.

An hour before, Frank had held her on that same landing. They had always found it so hard to leave each other.

Please don't give up on me, Frank, she prayed now. Please don't stop wanting me.

She had lost track of who didn't want to touch whom.

He hadn't been able to keep his hands off her back then.

"Frank, for goodness' sake," she would say when she felt his hand under her dress as they sat drinking outside at the restaurant where she worked. They had giggled like fools there on the patio next to the mock orange blossoms.

He had seemed solid to her and she wanted him to pass some of that along to her.

If only I knew how to love him properly, she thought now. If only I were someone else—a motherly sort of person—baking banana bread with a smile on my face and laughing over the back fence. Oh God. Denise groaned out loud. I'm never going to be up to raising three children, all at once. How did I let this happen?

Wim Winston walked onto the ward and pulled the curtain around her bed. He kissed her on the mouth and she said, "Wim, for Christ's sake."

"Let's go for a walk." He ran his hands up and down her arms. He didn't seem to question that she was his for the taking.

Denise elbowed him roughly and crossed her arms in front of her chest. "Leave me alone, Wim."

"Come on, Denise. Let's go."

"Are you supposed to even be here?"

"I can be anywhere I want to be."

He touched her again, this time on the inside of her thigh. Just a quick touch. She slapped him this time.

He laughed.

"If you don't go away right now, I'm going to start screaming," she said.

"Okay, okay, take it easy." He pulled the curtain back and vanished as quickly as he came.

Denise wondered if anything in life was for real. Were all the people that ran things as ridiculous as Wim Winston? In a way she hoped so and in another way it infuriated her because she had missed out on such a giant joke for so long.

Imagine him behaving that way right in the middle of a hospital ward!

She recalled there being something of the exhibitionist in Wim back when they had carried on together. In fact, that was probably part of what had attracted her to him. And there was something coiled and dangerous in Wim.

Once, fully clothed and standing, he had fucked her against the filthy outside wall of a downtown hotel. The Royal Albert Arms. It had been fun. Her feet had climbed the opposite wall till she was wedged between two buildings.

"Does that feel good?" He had gripped her wrists and spread her arms wide against the filthy bricks, like a scrunched up sideways Jesus Christ.

"Does it feel good when I fuck you?" he had asked.

She had known better even then than to give him the satisfaction of an answer.

And she felt a small amount of pride in herself now at the memory.

CHAPTER 30

After work Frank sat in the parking lot of the police station with his car window rolled down. He didn't want to go home because Denise wasn't there. He didn't want to go to the hospital because Denise was there.

He drove south down St. Mary's Road till he came to Kingston Row. The station wagon was dragging again. It drove as though the emergency brake was on. He knew well enough what that felt like.

I must get it in for servicing, Frank thought.

He turned onto Kingston Crescent. This was his favourite street. He parked at the Elm Park Bridge and walked over to the Bridge Drive-In.

Guilt tempered his anticipation; his kids should be here for this. He wouldn't be able to tell them. They'd lose their minds. He thought of going home to get them and then threw caution to the wind and sidled into the line-up for his first milkshake of the season.

He drove toward the hospital savouring the taste of chocolate and thinking about his encounter with Ivy Srutwa-Grace. He had finally been able to get her to sit down but then wished he hadn't when she made it seem like the chair in Frank's office was somehow making her dirty, interfering with her coat and hands. She wouldn't touch anything, even with those gloves—thin leather gloves—for driving he supposed.

Frank didn't want to be a part of whatever it was she was up to. He was pretty sure it was some sort of game Ivy was playing, but he wasn't positive and he couldn't just brush her off.

"I've offered myself up," she'd said, "to help track people down for the Nelson Mac reunion and I'm afraid I'm not making out very well. It's been ages since I've had anything to do with that community. I don't really know anything except what I'm able to find in the phone book."

"How did you find me?" Frank asked.

"Oh. I heard you had become a policeman years ago. You weren't at all hard to find with that big of a clue. Anyway, I figured with your being with the police and still living in Norwood that you'd probably have a line on far more people than I do."

"How did you know I still live in Norwood?" Frank knew he was babbling.

"You're in the phone book, Frank. Even your first name. Didn't anyone ever teach you that's a bad idea? Claremont Avenue. Just a few streets over from where you grew up. You must really like the neighbourhood."

Frank was panicking inside. Everything she said seemed two-edged, sharp as knives. But the whole spiel was cushioned in her fresh scent and her apparent guilelessness. Anyone else uttering the same words and Frank would be day dreaming. She held him riveted, motionless with alarm.

Suddenly his head grew too heavy for his neck and he had to support it with his hands.

"I hope it's not asking too much. I'm sure you're a very busy man."

She looked around the room and her eyes rested on a picture of Emma, Garth and Sadie on his desk.

"Are those your children?" she asked.

"Yes." Frank picked up the photograph and held it to his chest. "Forgive me, Ivy, but…"

"What, Frank? What is it?"

"Well it's just, I know I'm a cop and all and that I live in the neighbourhood, but still…why me? I mean you must have terrible memories of me. I can't believe you'd want to be in the same room with me."

He knew what her answer would be and knew it was wrong. It was crazy.

"Because you were nice," she said.

"Oh, Ivy. God help me. God help you. I wasn't nice!"

She thought he was nice. He wanted to hit her over the head with a piece of lumber. Maybe that would convince her that he wasn't. He wished she were dead. He wished he were dead.

"God help us all," he said.

Ivy smiled. "I saw you as good. I mean, relatively speaking, you were. What you did. What you didn't do. You were just a kid after all."

Frank cringed. "Please don't make excuses for me, Ivy. I do enough of that for myself."

He walked to the window and looked out at the bench where he had sat several days ago, way back before Ivy had walked into his office. He had thought he had troubles then. That time looked positively idyllic from where he stood now. All he'd had on his plate was an alcoholic wife and an urge to do a little wandering.

He heard her voice behind him, but he had stopped listening. He was thinking about the Simkins, Dwight and Duane—Greta Bower's stepbrothers. They had been there. Duane was the worst, no question.

"I'd be happy to help you, Ivy," Frank said, turning to face her.

"Good! Thank you, Frank." Ivy smiled.

Frank smiled back as best he could.

"Let's meet somewhere nicer to talk about it, shall we?" she said. "Like The Forks."

She stood up to leave. "I'll make a list of the people I'm having trouble tracking down and bring it along. I didn't want to presume too much by bringing it this time." She smiled again.

"Call me then, Ivy, and we'll set something up."

Frank saw her to the door and then sat down behind his desk. He felt heavy, as though seeing Ivy Srutwa had added forty pounds to his body weight.

He hauled out his wool and began to knit.

Now Frank was sitting in the parking lot of the hospital, finishing his milkshake. He made loud slurping sounds through his straw to get every last bit, the kind of sounds he was always telling his kids not to make because it was bad manners.

Frank was confused. What was Ivy up to? He knew there was a Nelson Mac reunion coming up in the fall but he was sure that her visit had nothing to do with that. Frank knew he had a reputation for being a little naive at times but even he wasn't thick enough to believe her community-minded cover story.

He left his car doors unlocked. That way there would be less physical damage if someone stole it.

He whistled "Happy Birthday" quietly to himself as he walked along toward the ancient building that housed the Chemical Withdrawal Unit. He was so tired of this.

CHAPTER 31
1965

Ivy doesn't make a sound. Nor does she struggle as the boy ties her wrists and ankles to the rough wood of the filthy penalty box. It's just the one boy doing the tying. Duane Simkin.

One of the other boys is nervous and says, "Come on, Duane. You don't have to tie her. It's not like she's gonna get away or anything."

Duane ignores him and yanks the rope tighter.

"I can't be a part of this," the nervous boy says.

"So fuck off, then," says Duane and the nervous boy is gone.

Her legs are spread so wide apart she feels as though her thighs will become detached from her body when he starts shoving himself inside her. Like the thighs that her mother rips away from the chicken body at Sunday supper.

She hears herself gasp as he rams himself home. The groans of the boy are louder than her own. He sounds like he is the one in pain.

Her legs remain intact though, through four boys and through the wooden hammer handle that the one named Duane pushes into her. That is the worst part. That is when she can feel herself tearing and knows there will be blood and trouble. She'll have slivers inside her. How will she ever get them out? Maybe it will be the slivers that kill her.

Her mother won't look at her but will make her chores harder than usual. Like going to visit her grandma, for instance, in the sour dark of her apartment.

"Rub Grandma's ankles," the old woman will croak and Ivy will take a thick foot in her lap and press the swollen flesh, dry as dusty cardboard.

She wonders now who will find her. It will have to come to that because there is no way in the world she'll be able to untie the knots. They're too tight.

In the end it's the nervous boy who lets her go. The one who was against tying her in the first place. He comes back.

"Sorry," he mutters as he cuts the ropes with his pocket knife.

"What?" Ivy can't believe her ears.

He doesn't have the wherewithal to say it again.

"Do you know anything about volcanoes?" Emma asked.

Donald sat leaning against a tree in front of the school. He was alone, which didn't happen very often, so Emma figured she'd speak to him even though his eyes were closed. After all, he'd touched her shoulder the other day. And looked at her while he did it. She had gone over it again and again in her mind. It was the best thing that had ever happened to her boy-wise. She loved that he had looked right at her when he touched her. That seemed so brave to her.

Donald opened his eyes and smiled. "Hi, Em."

"Hi."

He smiled some more and she admired his silence.

"Well, do ya?" she said.

"Do I what?" he asked.

"Know anything about volcanoes?"

"Oh. Well, a little bit, I guess. I know about Mount St. Helens."

"What's Mount St. Helens?"

"It's a volcano. Sit down. I can't see you properly looking into the sun."

Emma sat and Donald told her what he knew about Mount St. Helens and Emma told him about her desire to make a volcano for her science project, one that could erupt. That would be the hard part, she said.

"What a great idea!" he said. "I'll help you if you want."

"That'd be great." Emma stood up. "I gotta go now or I'll be late."

"Late for what?"

"Oh, I've got this thing."

She didn't have a thing, but she was too nervous to sit with him any longer.

"See ya, Donald." She said his name out loud. She made herself do it and was glad she did. Up till now she hadn't thought about people's names as anything other than what people were called. But now they seemed magic. The word Donald was magic, and even more so when spoken aloud. And her name, Em, when Donald said it, made her feel the way she had felt when he touched her the other day. It did the same thing to the inside of her.

"Okay, I'll see ya then, Em," he said. "Let's get together soon to talk about your volcano."

"Okay." She smiled as she backed away. "See ya."

I'm the happiest girl in the world, Emma thought. I love Donald Griffiths and I'm pretty sure he likes me. I said his name out loud and he said mine and we're gonna talk some more about volcanoes.

"I love volcanoes," she said.

Emma phoned Delia to tell her what had happened.

"What're ya, mental?" Delia asked when Emma got to the part about how she got up and left him there under the tree. "You shoulda like, played it out, you crazy idiot. He might have walked you home or made a date or kissed you or something."

"I couldn't, Dele. I couldn't take anymore just then. It's okay what I did. It all feels perfect to me."

Emma caught a glimpse of herself in the mirror as she talked to her friend. She liked what she saw and stared amazed, as this animated girl with colour in her cheeks gestured and smiled and lived a life. She hoped that this was what she had looked like when she had been talking to Donald.

The trouble with mirrors, she realized, when she hung up the phone and was left with a quiet picture of herself, was that they caught you at your dullest. Who looks nice when they're gazing stupidly and self-absorbedly into the mirror looking for pimples? Maybe movie stars like Winona Ryder and Claire Danes, but no normal people.

Emma stretched out on her bed and reviewed the newest Donald experience in her mind. Then she went over the one again when he touched her shoulder. If she had to pick, she'd pick that one.

CHAPTER 33

It was twilight and Gus prepared for a seeding. He placed the bag of birdseed beside him on the car seat and headed out. It wouldn't be hard to find what he was looking for. There were men at work everywhere these days: on sidewalks, city roads, private driveways, and parking lots. They were correcting the damage from the winter frost and the years of wear and tear, laying new cement, smoothing it with their special equipment, and then leaving it precariously guarded with barricades. Sometimes on private property there would be a flimsy piece of cardboard with an invitation: KEEP OFF.

He didn't have to travel very far tonight to find a good spot. It was a driveway right on the street where he lived, towards the park end. Two guys were still at it so he drove to the end of the block and sat awhile waiting for them to finish up. This was perfect. It was important that the cement be wet.

In the fading light he drove the old Buick back to the freshly poured driveway. It was easy; he could manage it without getting out of the car. Behind his open door he sowed a careful layer of birdseed on the gentle slope that joined the new driveway with the city street. And then he drove away.

Ivy watched from behind her tinted glass. She could remember going as a kid to these magic play sites and carefully printing her name in the fresh cement to leave her mark. Back then she had imagined herself as a grown woman coming back to her home town and seeking out her name in the cement. She had invented nostalgia for herself and marveled at the achy wonder of it.

Ivy didn't like the old man. He was her enemy and she'd known it from the first time she saw him; she suspected he knew it too. She shouldn't have spoken to him the other evening. What did she say? Whatever it was it was too much and she should have known better. It had caused him to notice her and she didn't want attention coming from the wrong person. She didn't want any interference.

"I probably scare him." She spoke to the stale air inside the car. "I scare myself sometimes."

Ivy rolled down her window after he drove off and was surprised at how dark it had become. Sometimes she wished she could live inside the light and change with it. Maybe then she wouldn't get so bored with the sameness of things.

CHAPTER 34

In the wee hours Emma lay awake. She rose from her bed and tiptoed over to the window. She felt expectant. It was something about the night.

The tall figure leaned against the lamppost, smoking in the drizzle. Emma stared. She would have been frightened if the man had stared back but he didn't. If indeed it was a man. There was a femaleness in the way he held the cigarette and shook his hair back off the pale blank oval that was his face.

Emma watched as the figure smoked in the glow from the street light. She wondered if he, or maybe she, was connected to her in some way. The person stood close enough to her bedroom window that she could smell the smoke. She hoped it had nothing to do with her.

Emma ran down the stairs and out the back door. By the time she crossed the yard the lane was empty. There wasn't even anyone disappearing down the alleyway.

It was just Emma and the rain. She shivered in the damp as she imagined what she must look like standing there by the lamppost, in its eerie glow. She was afraid to look up at her bedroom window in case she saw her own face gazing down.

In the morning Emma asked her dad to join her on her paper route.

They ran into Rupe and the fluffy dog named Easy and Emma introduced them to her father.

"Isn't Easy great!" she said. "I just love the way he carries himself."

Rupe and Frank smiled at each other.

They passed the Marlboro Man and Emma pointed him out.

She told her dad about the slow-driving car and last night in the drizzle and they talked again about getting a dog.

By the time the paper wagon was empty Frank had agreed to take her to the Humane Society to pick out a pup—real soon.

CHAPTER 35

Ivy placed the handcuffs in her bag of pointed objects. They must have come from Frank's workplace but she couldn't remember.

I hope I haven't been putting myself at risk, she thought. How can I be careful if I'm not there?

She did recall Frank being very preoccupied with himself—so much so she probably could have stolen the shoes off his feet and he wouldn't have noticed.

Ivy drove to Brookside Cemetery on the north side of the city. She was going to visit her brother Ray, who died thirty-four summers ago.

She pictured him beneath the ground, gone to dust. His grave was in the children's section. She watched a young couple in their good clothes putting flowers on a grave a few rows over. They huddled together for comfort. Their child. Ivy's eyes met those of the mother and the woman smiled sadly, willing to share her pain with a stranger who she probably thought mourned her own baby.

Ivy did that once, but it was a very long time ago.

She turned away and stared at the ground. She had a picture of Ray in her head. It didn't look anything like the photograph behind plastic in her wallet. She took it out and looked at it. He was fourteen years old in the photo. It was a school picture. His hair was slicked back with Wild Root Cream Oil. Ivy remembered the smell.

Ray wasn't smiling in the photograph, so he looked better in her mind's eye. There he always had a smile. She had a sense of him now and then—a morning feeling that came over her in the summer sometimes, when she glimpsed a section of unpaved road or a patch of grass long enough to bend in the wind.

And she had his face in her mind's eye.

When Ivy looked up again she saw the geezer from last night. Frank's next-door neighbour. He leaned over what looked to be a new grave and placed a handful of crocuses on it.

This isn't a good sign, thought Ivy, not a good sign at all.

It was important that the old crow not see her, but it was too late. He looked at her and recognition flickered across his weathered face. He glanced at her Lincoln parked on the road in front of his old Buick. And then back at her.

Ivy waved and he nodded his head in acknowledgement. He didn't want to; worry creased his face, like ruts in a dirt road.

Rightly so, thought Ivy. Rightly so.

She envied the dead children in the graveyard. How easy it was for them! To be loved and treasured so, before they were old enough to start messing up and doing all the things that would make people hate them and run from them. Like the old man wanted to run from her now. The love for the dead children would never waver. It had nothing to do with the people they would have become.

Families of geese scratched about on the banks of the creek that ran through the graveyard. Mothers fussed over their young ones in an annoyingly human way as Ivy approached. Counting the geese was hard because new ones kept swimming out of the reeds or waddling over from further down the creek. And then she wouldn't know if the ones she had already counted were the same ones or entirely new. It reminded her of something and she felt a roiling in her guts.

She took out her notebook to record the number of birds. One tear splatted onto the page and smudged the marks she had made there. For a terrible moment the uselessness of her act slipped through her line of vision, like a quick view of a squashed movie title that occupied only the central portion of the screen. Then it was gone.

She sat with the geese until a maintenance truck parked too close. Three men got out and began the noisy job of trimming trees, keeping things nice and neat for the dead.

As Ivy walked back to her car she thought about Frank's daughter, Emma. She'd heard the geezer call the girl by name. She's a pretty thing, Ivy thought, tiny, waif-like. Ivy didn't like that Frank had a photograph of his kids on his desk. And she hated that he had picked it up and held it to his chest as though he had to protect it from her. Frank had good instincts. He just wasn't too bright and had a lot on his mind.

The old man's Buick was gone. Good.

Ivy was confused. She knew she was going to have to get her thoughts in some kind of order. Gruck had vanished without a trace, abandoned ship, left her in the lurch. Between no G and the voice called Reuben and the muddled Squeaks, she felt as though everything she was working towards might fall to pieces around her.

Her project had become complicated. It had different fields now, when before it had only the one, to do with the men. The edges of the fields were fluid. They flowed into one another and blurred, like water colours applied too soon, and she had difficulty keeping them separate.

There was Emma, for instance. Her pixie face loomed just outside Ivy's peripheral vision, day and night. She lived inside Ivy's right temple, larger than life or death. The Emma task had grown bigger than the man task and Ivy didn't know how that had happened. She suspected it was connected to the Squeaks.

And there was a smell that came. It had to do with dying and something left alone too long. Ivy had known it in her youth and now it came again. It upset her and disturbed her sleep. The death smell wove itself into her dreams and lurched her awake till she lay slippery with fear in the darkness of her lonely room.

The voice called Reuben had led her there and she felt betrayed. She had felt protected by the voice and now it led her where she least wanted to go. To Olive Srutwa, her mother.

Ivy hadn't thought of her in years and didn't want to think of her now. Was she still alive? Somehow, Ivy knew that she was.

She prayed for her plan to stop expanding. If she could just stay on one course long enough to complete one thing, she felt sure the other things would be easier. It was all getting so complicated.

She turned to a clean page in her notebook and wrote: Task at Hand: Do the men.

Then the Squeaks began.

They made her drive to the community club, the one with the spire in the distance. She looked for something familiar. The building had been replaced but the grounds were pretty much the same. Except the pleasure rink had become a parking lot. The two hockey rinks were there with their spring grass and boards and penalty boxes. Still the same.

Ivy walked over to one of the boxes and saw plywood on the floor, covered with a heavy black rubber mat. The dirt of her youth had been covered over. And the walls were new and painted white. No slivers here. No nails sticking out and digging in.

When the Squeaks stopped, Ivy was behind the wheel of her Lincoln turning right off Main Street in the direction of The Forks. She looked at her watch. Noon. She was right on time for her meeting with Frank Foote.

CHAPTER 36
1966

Ivy has never known such pain. Even when the boys raped her in the penalty box it didn't hurt this much.

Olive forces gin down her throat, but it doesn't help. She is ruined.

She loved the life inside her regardless of how it came to be. For as long as no one knew, it was her reason for being. It sustained her. He did. Ivy thinks of the baby as a he. A he to run away with and love. And then he would love her in return someday. But she didn't run soon enough.

Now he's in a plastic bag within a paper bag. In her mother's hands.

"I'll leave the gin here on your night stand," Olive says. "Drink as much as you want. I'm going out for a few minutes."

Ivy doesn't want to drink. She wants to feel the pain as long as she can. It's her only connection.

I should have run sooner, she thinks. If only I had run sooner.

The names of the boys who hurt Ivy were almost as deeply etched in Frank's brain as they must be in hers. They resided there as clearly as his guilt at the front of his mind. He even knew what had become of all of them.

"Wim Winston." Frank read from the list of names Ivy had pushed across the table towards him. Her list was long, but that was the first name that jumped out at him.

"Pardon?"

"Wim Winston. " Frank pulled out his handkerchief and wiped his brow. He had started to sweat.

"That's a stupid name," Ivy said.

"Yeah it is, isn't it?" Frank chuckled nervously. "I guess it's short for something. Wimston, maybe. Wimston Winston." Maybe she didn't know that Wim had been one of the guys. Or didn't remember? No. She was messing with his head.

Ivy laughed. It sounded real. It was the first time Frank had heard this and it relaxed him a little. Maybe she wasn't so completely weird if she could laugh.

"Don't worry about that name. I already figured out where he is. He's a doctor, I believe, here in Winnipeg?"

"Yes." Frank stared at Ivy's eyes but there was nothing there for him to see.

They were sitting at an outdoor bar at The Forks where the Assiniboine and Red rivers met. It was a wonderful place to be but it was ruined for Frank by the business at hand: this Nelson McIntyre high school reunion business.

Ivy looked more like someone who was infiltrating a committee investigating the illegal activity of a government agency than a woman planning her high school reunion. Her high school days must have been a nightmare for her, judging from the little Frank knew of them. He wanted to say: What are you really up to? But he didn't.

He sipped a beer and perused the names. Ivy had compiled the list and written it out in her own hand. Some people Frank knew, some he knew of, some didn't ring a bell at all. The boys were all there: Wim, Duane, Dwight, Fat Ronnie. Their names were interspersed with the others. What was this about?

Frank had no recollection of about half the people on the list. He helped her as best he could with those he knew were still around. He talked about others who were dead and some who had moved away. Frank had heard a terrible story about Ronnie Fowler, so he figured he may as well share it with Ivy.

"Ron is the eighteenth fattest man in the world," he said.

"What?"

"I ran into his sister a couple of years ago. Ron lives in Mississauga with his mother now, has for some years. She tried to get him into the *Guinness Book of World Records*, but of course, at eighteenth, he didn't qualify."

Ivy stared at Frank.

"I don't think he's going to be coming to any reunions," Frank said. "They can't even get him out of the house."

"Sad," said Ivy.

"Yes," said Frank.

He went through the list in order, told her the fate of the Simkin brothers, and watched as she entered the information in her notebook. She printed in an awkward backhand, her tongue curled out the side of her mouth. Like Frank's son, Garth, who was left-handed. But Ivy wasn't left-handed—she just wrote oddly. She pressed so lightly with her pencil that the words were barely discernible from Frank's side of the table. He wondered why she used a pencil and why she wrote so feebly.

But there wasn't much about this woman that didn't baffle him. He didn't want to have to try to figure her out. Maybe she would disappear as suddenly as she came. He doubted it.

"So they don't live here anymore," Ivy said. "The Simkin boys."

"No."

She was connected to the rain barrel baby. He was sure of it. But how? And why on earth would she present herself to him in this way, knowing he was a cop?

When he got to the particulars of it, his mind clouded over. He was too far inside it, too far inside the past. He needed to talk to someone who could help him see more clearly, see things as they really were.

Who could he tell, without bringing up what happened to Ivy in the penalty box all those years ago? This was turning into a nightmare. How could he have thought it wouldn't eventually catch up to him? He hadn't thought that, he realized now. He had always known it would.

Frank didn't know what Ivy's plan was. But he did know he had to go along with the high school reunion charade until he figured out what to do. He couldn't let her get away, much as he would love to never lay eyes on her again.

Frank gave his head a shake. He tried to picture this woman dropping a dead baby into a rain barrel. He couldn't. And what would she be doing with a baby anyway? Beautiful though she was, she was a little long in the tooth for a newborn baby. Still, it wasn't impossible.

If placing the baby in the rain barrel was revenge it was a particularly evil one. Sick. Worse than a horse's head in the bed. Especially when it was only poor Greta who lived in the Simkin house now. Her brothers weren't even there to receive it. It was a roundabout revenge. Limp, but ghastly.

Maybe Ivy had nothing to do with the baby at all. It had just been so fresh in his mind when she appeared on the scene that he had leapt to an unlikely conclusion.

Like Fred said, she seemed nice. Somewhat odd, but nice. And she didn't strike him as the type that would want to make a big deal out of things. There was a stillness about her.

Maybe she just wanted to confront her past in some way. She had heard about the reunion and figured that might be a good starting point. Maybe she had joined a twelve-step group and was at the confronting stage. Denise had gone through that during one of the times she had joined AA. She had gone around apologizing to people for things that they didn't remember that she had said or done. It made her feel better for a few minutes. Maybe it was something like that, but the opposite. Maybe Ivy was looking for apologies or explanations. Or blood.

Frank thought again about the tiny creature found in Greta's backyard. He couldn't very well say: "So, had any babies lately?" He could ask: "Do you have any children, Ivy?" And he did.

"No," was all she said.

A warm breeze threatened to blow away their cocktail napkins and Frank anchored them with their drinks. Ivy's was a Perrier, which didn't surprise him. He had taken her for a mineral water type, one who would want to keep her wits about her at all times.

"How old are your children, Frank?" Ivy asked.

"Thirteen, eight and six." He didn't want to tell her about his kids. He wished he had lied about their ages.

"This has been a big help." Ivy closed her notebook. "Can I leave the list with you just in case you come up with something else?"

"Of course."

Frank knew he couldn't help Ivy any more. She had everything she needed from him and they both knew it. All the boys were on her list and most of them were out of reach. He didn't have to worry about Dwight: he was dead. Or Duane: he was safe in jail. And he was pretty sure he didn't have to be concerned about Ronnie.

But what about Wim? There was no love lost between Frank Foote and Wim Winston. But Frank wondered now if he should try to warn him in some way, much as he found the very idea of him distasteful. But warn him of what exactly? Ivy Srutwa's in town. So what?

On the path between the patio and the river a dog and his master stepped smartly. Frank recognized the pair Emma had introduced him to that morning, Easy and his master. He forgot the master's name.

The man saw Frank and waved. Then he saw Ivy and blanched. Ivy saw him and called, "Hello there."

"Do you know his name?" Frank asked. "I really should know his name."

"No," Ivy said. "I never find out their names if I can help it."

A gust of wind rustled through the patio area. People jumped to rescue papers and to brush hair away from their faces. Ivy's hair didn't move. It was locked in place around her smooth tight lovely face.

CHAPTER 38

Gus sauntered down the street to see if his handiwork of the night before had met with success. It had. The bird seed was gone and the birds' feet had left a dainty pattern in the hard new cement.

Gus smiled and shouted, "Good afternoon!" to a man in a suit standing further on up the driveway.

He recalled the footprints of seagulls in the sand at Gimli. There and gone, there and gone. Well, it would be some time before these particular footprints disappeared and Gus chuckled as he strolled back down the street toward home.

He had worried at first that the birds would have problems with cement attaching itself to their feet. But they were almost weightless and even if a tiny bit did stick it would soon wear itself off. And he figured the amount of cement attached to a few seeds swallowed by one bird at one feed wouldn't account for any digestive trouble. He sowed in a different spot each time so it was unlikely the same bird would ever feed twice. And he was sure they were no strangers to what was really just a bit of sand and gravel and water mixed up together, maybe a bit of clay and limestone thrown in. Hell, they probably ate that stuff all the time, just not in these precise proportions.

Yesterday morning Gus had overheard the caretaker at the community club talking about replacing the sidewalk between the two hockey rinks. Apparently it was going to happen some time this summer. He'd have to keep his eyes open for that.

CHAPTER 39

Frank sat at his desk and tried to concentrate on the reports in front of him. He was supposed to be filling out evaluations of two new patrol sergeants working under him but he didn't know them well enough yet.

His mind kept wandering back to Ivy Grace. He knew he had to act; it would be irresponsible not to.

His hunch, that Ivy had put the baby in the barrel in Greta's yard, was based on his intimate knowledge of the details of her rape thirty years ago. And on his knowledge that Greta was the stepsister of two of the boys who instigated and participated in that rape.

Frank's insides heaved when he pictured the wild-eyed brothers that he saw too much of for a while back then. Poor Greta'd had to share a house with them.

The rape was never reported, never punished, never avenged. If Frank was to pursue his hunch he would have to admit out loud to someone, to Fred, to Superintendent Flagston, probably eventually to the newspaper and therefore his family, what he hadn't been capable of stopping all those years ago. It was the greatest shame of his life.

He didn't want to share his past with Fred. Fred looked up to him and Frank didn't want to watch that respect drain out of his sergeant's face before his very eyes.

Also Fred could be very gung-ho and Frank didn't want this getting away on him.

He had stopped stewing over whether it was Ivy's own baby or someone else's, whether she had killed it herself or found it dead.

It was Ivy's baby, her very own. Frank knew it. He had talked himself into it.

He knew he had to discuss it with someone and the only person he could think of that made any sense at all was his boss, Ed Flagston.

He had to get some feedback. Maybe this was some wild tangent he was on and he just needed Ed to get him back on track. Maybe he was crazy. He sure hoped so.

Ed was his guy. He wouldn't blab, judge, or jump to unlikely conclusions. Sometimes Frank wished he could be Ed Flagston, with his cool head and compartmentalized way of looking at things. But he wouldn't want to smoke a pack of Export A's a day or have a gut that hung as far over his belt as Ed's did. Ed called it "Dunlop's Disease": My stomach dun lops right over my belt! he was fond of saying.

Frank set aside his reports and walked down the hall to his boss's office. Ed wasn't there. He was at his daughter's graduation exercises, and according to his secretary, Brian, there was a huge celebration afterwards so he wouldn't likely be back.

"Is it important, sir?" Brian asked. "I could probably track him down."

"No, Brian. Don't worry about it. I'll catch him tomorrow sometime."

"Would you like to make an appointment?" Brian asked. "That might be best. Tomorrow afternoon, say? Three-thirty?"

"Thanks, Brian. That'd be fine."

Back in his office, Frank left a message on Wim Winston's voice mail.

CHAPTER 40

"He's like, 'Have you seen Emma today?' and I'm like, 'Yeah, we walked to school together,' and he goes, 'Do you know where she is now?' and I'm like, 'No,' and…"

"Delia, wait!" Emma said. "Okay, stop walking. I'll be you and you be him. Now tell me exactly what he said. Okay, I'm you: 'Hi Donald! What's shakin'?'"

"I wouldn't say, 'What's shakin'?'"

"Okay. I'm you. 'Hi, Don. How's it goin'?'"

"I wouldn't call him Don. No one calls him Don."

"Oh God, Dele. Okay. 'Hi, Donald. How's it goin'?'"

"Okay. 'Hi, Delia. Not bad. Have you seen Emma today?'"

"'Yeah. We walked to school together.'"

"'Do you, like, know where she is now?'"

"He wouldn'ta said 'like.'"

"Okay. 'Do ya know where she is now?'"

"Okay. 'No.'"

"'Well, if you see her, could you tell her I'm lookin' for her?' And then he smiled and that was it."

"Oh God. This is so great." Emma sat down in the middle of the sidewalk and looked up at her friend.

"What did he look like when he smiled?"

"Well, just kind of normal but with a smile on his face."

"Did he look beautiful?"

"He looked cute, I guess. I wouldn't say beautiful. Stand up, you idiot. People are staring at you."

Emma lay down.

"I love him so much I think I'm gonna throw up."

"Snap out of it," Delia said.

"I can't."

"Here he comes!"

Emma scrambled to her feet.

"Just kidding!" Delia took off, running.

Emma chased her down the street, shrieking, "I'm gonna kill you!"

Delia shrieked back, "It was for your own good!"

On a June afternoon in 1966 no one bothers Ivy Srutwa. She gazes out the open classroom window at the street beyond. The perfume of purple lilacs floats in on the summer breeze. She hears a train blowing its whistle from across the Red River. It threatens to drown out the voice of her history teacher, Mr. Friesen, droning on about the Battle of Hastings, fought in 1066.

She stands up, inside the lilac scent, and moves toward the door. One or two people watch the motion from a lazy place behind their eyes. Most don't notice.

She walks down the lanes in the shimmering heat of early afternoon till she comes to the stifling bungalow she shares with her mother and her older brother Wilf.

She walks by Olive, who sits at the kitchen table smoking and playing solitaire. The stink of old gin rises from her mother. Gin and something else.

Ivy walks down the cellar stairs.

It was here that her father took his own life. He threw a rope over a beam and stood on a chair. He fastened that rope around his own neck and kicked the chair out from under him. All of this before Ivy was born. It was what Duane Simkin had been talking about when he taunted her about her dad being in hell. It was what Frank Foote had been referring to when he told Duane to shut up about her dad. Other people had known about it when Ivy hadn't.

Olive told her about it, finally, one day when Ivy kept asking her about his spells.

"Did he know I existed?" Ivy asked. "Did he know that you were pregnant with me?"

"Sure he knew. Whaddya think?" Olive said. "Anyway, what difference does all that make at this point? Have you run out of garbage to write about in your brother's old scribblers?"

Ivy gathered up the notebooks she had hidden under her mattress. She couldn't bear knowing that her mother had been a witness to her secret self. At the river she lit a fire. She ripped her words to shreds and fed them to the flames.

In the cellar now Ivy finds a small cloth suitcase that someone once said belonged to her father. She heads back upstairs.

Her mother speaks but Ivy doesn't listen.

She places some clothes and a few items from the bathroom inside the musty bag.

Olive shouts now, but Ivy still doesn't listen.

She pauses at the front door but doesn't turn around. She walks out, cloth bag in hand, and lets the screen door slam behind her.

As she walks up St. Mary's Road toward downtown she thinks of all the fine things she's never done and maybe never will do, but can, if she puts herself in the right places and changes a little.

She's almost finished grade ten.

The Battle of Hastings was fought in 1066.

CHAPTER 42
The Present

"Donald Griffiths is coming over to help me work on my volcano."

"Who's Donald Griffiths?" Frank asked.

"He's a guy in my class and he knows about volcanoes and things." Emma added more Harvest Crunch to her bowl to even out with the milk that was left over.

Emma's having a boy over, Frank thought. Life as we know it is finished.

"When's he coming? Will I get to meet him, I hope?"

"He's coming after supper tonight. I figured we could work up in my room. That's where all my stuff is."

That's also where your bed is, and your pajamas and your underwear drawer, thought Frank.

"I think maybe for tonight you should set things up here in the kitchen," he said. "I don't know if Donald...Donald who?"

"Griffiths."

"I don't know if Donald Griffiths is ready for your bedroom, Em."

"I cleaned it up specially."

"Still, I think Donald's parents and I would be more comfortable if you worked in the kitchen tonight."

Frank got up to pour himself more coffee. There was no cream.

"He only has a mum," Emma said. "What about Garth and Sadie and everyone? They'll be all over us and embarrassing me and everything."

"I'll make you a deal." Frank poured milk into his coffee and took a sip. "Yuck! I've got to pick up some groceries. I hate milk in coffee."

"You shouldn't be drinking cream," Emma said. "It's bad for you."

"Yeah, but I like it. It agrees with me." Frank added cream to the grocery list on the fridge, removed the yellow paper from under its cow magnet and stuck it in his shirt pocket.

"Anyway," he said, "the deal is, I'll try my best to keep Garth and Sadie out of your hair if you'll work on your volcano in the kitchen tonight."

"Aw, Dad."

"I think that's reasonable, Em."

"Yeah, all right then."

"Great! I look forward to meeting this Donald."

"Yeah, great."

"Would you like to come up to the hospital with me later to see your mum?" Frank asked.

"Mmm, no, I don't think so," Emma said.

"Are you sure? I think she'd really like to see you."

"I hate her," Emma said quietly.

"Oh, Emma. No you don't."

"Yeah. I do, Dad. I really do."

She rinsed her bowl and placed it neatly with the other dishes beside the sink. When Denise was away the rules were loosened up some and the dishes were just washed once at the end of the eating day. It suited everyone till evening rolled around.

"Believe it or not," Frank said, "your mother is trying her hardest right now."

"I don't believe it," Emma replied.

Frank slouched over the kitchen table long after she had left for school. She was punishing Denise. For not loving her correctly, Frank supposed, in a way that would have been acceptable to Emma. And of course, for being a drunkard. The two went hand in hand. He hadn't known how to handle her statement of hatred. He wondered what Gus would have thought of that particular bit of parenting.

CHAPTER 43

The phone message in Wim Winston's hand was shaking. Frank
Foote wanted him to call and Wim's secretary had written "ASAP"
beside the number.

"Jesus."

He knew he had to return the call. Denise was a patient in his
hospital and Frank was her husband. Maybe Frank just wanted to ask
him to look in on her, see how she was getting along. See if, in Wim's
professional opinion, she was going to turn things around this time.
Quit drinking once and for all. Sure thing, Frank.

Wim punched in the numbers. Maybe Denise hadn't told on
him. Maybe Frank wasn't calling in order to set up a date to kill him
for coming on to his wife.

Frank answered on the first ring.

"Wim. Thanks for returning my call. Could we get together do
you suppose? This isn't something I want to talk about over the
phone."

She told him, Wim thought. But he sounds more tense than mad.
Maybe he wants to plead with me to leave her alone. That would be
even worse. You can never tell with a cop. I shouldn't have bothered
with her.

CHAPTER 44

Frank sat in Ed Flagston's outer office listening to Brian recite his recipe for flank steak to someone over the phone. Frank's stomach growled. The only thing he'd eaten all day was a piece of Greta Bower's rhubarb pie at a coffee shop down the street from the police station.

Flagston opened his door and motioned for him to come in.

"How's it going, Frank? Have a seat."

The room was thick with cigarette smoke and Frank longed to open a window.

"Pretty good. Thanks, Ed."

"What can I do for you? How are your guys getting along with the rain barrel case?"

Ed leaned over his fish tank. He sprinkled in a little food and Frank watched ash fall from his cigarette into the water. He wondered how the fish liked their home.

"Actually, that's what I'd like to talk to you about. As I'm sure you're aware, we've pretty much hit a brick wall. But something has come up in my private life that I have an uncomfortable feeling about. And I think it may be connected to little Jane Doe."

Ed sat down behind his desk and gave Frank his full attention.

"Ed, I've come to ask your advice. I feel buried in this thing and I can't see straight. What I'm about to tell you is something I'm not proud of. God, this is hard!"

"Frank. Look at me."

Frank met Ed's eyes and saw nothing but kindness and patience.

"This is between the two of us," Ed said.

"Thank you. I know I can't expect any kind of special treatment."

"You're a good man, Frank," Ed said, "and a good cop. Now tell me."

Frank began in 1965 with the gang rape of Ivy Srutwa. He explained how peripheral he'd been. He didn't take part. It was important that Ed know he didn't take part. And he had set poor young Ivy free, but not nearly soon enough. That was his crime.

He named the Simkin brothers. They were the ones that connected Ivy to the rain barrel. He told his boss that the Simkin boys used to live in Greta Bower's house. That they were her stepbrothers. That's where they lived at the time of Ivy's rape. And she would have known that.

"I hadn't seen her since high school," Frank went on. "She quit and disappeared. Till a few days ago when she walked into my office and asked me to help her track people down for our high school reunion."

"Nelson Mac?" Ed said.

"Yeah."

"I got my invitation already."

"Don't tell me you went there too."

"Sure did. Probably about ten years before you did. '53 to '57 it was.

"Jesus."

"Yeah. Small world."

Frank sat for a moment digesting this new information: Ed Flagston as a teenager roaming the same halls as Frank had, sneaking out for smokes, chasing girls in flared poodle skirts.

"You didn't stay like I did," Frank said.

"No. We like Crescentwood. I couldn't get out of Norwood fast enough, to tell you the truth. It's too much like a small town, everyone in your pocket. It suits some. Not me."

"I've mostly liked it pretty well," Frank said. "Till now."

"Go on with your story, Frank." Ed coughed, a terrible sound.

"Can we open a window, Ed, get some fresh air in here?"

"Sorry, Frank. I'm allergic to something out there at this time of year. It just about kills me."

Frank wanted to shake his boss, take his package of Export A's and stomp them into the ground.

He continued. "Well anyway, the Simkins were on the list of names Ivy wants me to help her track down. That's too weird. At first, I thought it was just the timing of Ivy's visit, when the rain barrel baby was still at the front of my mind, that made me unable to think of one incident separate from the other. But now I have this idea that it was a revenge ploy on her part, to get back at the boys who hurt her all those years ago. That little Jane Doe was her baby. It's just, she doesn't seem insane to me. Odd, but not crazy…I don't think." Frank leaned back in his chair. "I just don't know, Ed."

"That's quite a story, Frank. And quite a theory."

"Yeah."

"What do you want to do?"

"Well, I was thinking I could get some DNA, maybe some saliva from a drinking glass or something. I could take her for a drink. Then we could send it in for a comparison to little Jane."

"Sounds reasonable."

"It'll take forever." Frank was groveling. He knew Ed had a brother-in-law who worked in the RCMP lab on Academy Road, where the analysis would be done.

"A few weeks," Ed said.

"What if she's dangerous?"

"It sounds like she is."

"Yeah."

Ed lit another cigarette and inhaled deeply. "It's just…well, this is all based on something that happened thirty years ago and your feeling that Ivy Grace is odd. I'm convinced, but it's way too slim for us to convince anyone else that we should arrest her. We'll have to do this on the sly."

Frank breathed a sigh of relief. "I prefer it this way. For purely selfish reasons. I'm not looking forward to that gang rape business coming out."

"Maybe it won't have to." Ed coughed again, this time so violently that Frank worried he would lose this man before he had a chance to trap Ivy.

"My brother-in-law works in the lab." Ed smiled from behind his handkerchief. "As I'm sure you know, Frank. Linda's younger brother. Why don't I do the paperwork? I'll put his name on it and I'll speak to him. That should help to move it along. And I'll tell him to keep it under his hat."

"I'm very grateful, Ed."

Frank pushed back his chair. "If Ivy is the mother, it means that she's HIV-positive."

"Yes," said Ed. "Maybe you should get in touch with these Simkin characters and have a talk with them."

"I can't," Frank said. "Duane's in prison in Quebec and Dwight's dead."

"Oh. Well, that takes care of that."

Frank couldn't decide whether or not to mention Wim Winston and his part in the long-ago assault on Ivy Srutwa. He decided not to for the moment, but knew he had done the right thing by getting in touch with Wim.

He stood up. "Thanks for this, Ed. I'll set up another meeting with her and figure out the best way to go about getting that saliva sample."

Ed walked him to the door. "Are you going to the reunion?" he asked.

"I doubt it," Frank said and slipped out. He could think of few things he'd rather do less. One of them, though, was seeing Ivy Srutwa again.

"Life isn't very pleasant lately," he said out loud.

"Pardon, sir?" It was Brian, looking up from the latest issue of *Canadian Living*.

"Nothing, Brian. Sorry. Just talking to myself."

Frank stopped at the Marion Street Safeway for groceries on his way home. He decided to make spaghetti for supper. That would please everyone.

He could hardly wait to see his kids.

After supper, Frank took advantage of the cool evening to get a little more work done on the garage. He had finished the scraping and was now filling holes with spackling paste—a much more pleasant job.

When he was done, he snapped the lid onto his patching mixture and rinsed his putty knife under the garden hose. Some of the holes in the old boards of his garage were so big they were going to need a second application of the spackle.

Frank sighed and headed into the house to see what his kids were up to, to make sure none of them went to bed with dirty necks.

CHAPTER 45

Frank thought about Emma and her slow-moving car and her sinister figure in the rain. Maybe the slow-moving car was no one and the sinister figure was just Donald Griffiths longing for Frank's daughter.

It was mid-morning on Friday, and Frank waited for Wim Winston in a booth at the Salisbury House. The coffee tasted great—too bad he couldn't enjoy it. It had been Wim's idea to meet at the Sals. Frank figured on talking to him at the hospital and visiting Denise at the same time, killing two birds with one stone. But Wim suggested meeting "on neutral territory" as he put it. Frank didn't know what he was talking about. But as he watched Wim's Mercedes pull into the parking lot, old feelings of dislike resurfaced.

Frank knew that Wim and Denise had had a relationship of some kind a long time ago. He didn't like to think about it. A good many years had passed but Frank couldn't see Wim without picturing them going at it together. It was an unsavoury picture. What she had ever seen in Wim was a mystery to Frank. He hadn't always looked as bad as he did now but he had never looked good. And he wasn't even nice. But then, Frank knew sides of Wim he hoped Denise didn't.

Frank watched as Wim slid into the booth across from him. He extended a clammy hand and Frank shook it.

"How are you, Frank?" Beads of sweat glistened on Wim's forehead.

"You look like you already know what I want to talk to you about," Frank said. "Do you want coffee or anything, Wim?"

"No. Thanks. Let's just get right to it, shall we?"

"Has Ivy been in touch with you then, Wim?"

"Who? What are you talking about?" Wim took a serviette from the dispenser and wiped his forehead, wreaking havoc on his comb-over.

Frank wished he had a pair of scissors and more of a don't-give-a-shit attitude.

"Ivy."

"Who?"

"Ivy Srutwa. Her name's actually Ivy Grace now, but you'd remember her as Ivy Srutwa."

Wim looked blank, except for the new beads of sweat that popped out to replace the old ones.

If he says "who?" again I'm going to slap him, Frank thought.

"Who?"

He kicked Wim underneath the table.

"Ow!"

"Good grief, Wim. The Srutwas. The poor family that lived at the south end of the dike. Everybody made fun of them when we were kids. There was a mother and a daughter and a couple of sons. One of them died, I think, and the other one was quite a bit older than us. The dad killed himself. It was mainly the mum and the girl. The girl was Ivy."

"I don't remember."

Frank wanted to kick him again. He saw from Wim's eyes that this was going to be impossible. He wasn't going to give an iota. Frank was certain that Wim knew exactly who he was talking about. But he wasn't going to play. Not now, not ever.

"Okay, Wim." Frank swallowed the rest of his coffee in one gulp. "Catch ya later then."

He drove his Toyota station wagon around the Perimeter Highway a ways. The car had started stalling. Maybe all it needed was the carbon blown out of the engine from time to time.

He had tried to warn Wim. Maybe not real hard. But hard enough. And anyway, Wim, the shithead, had never heard of anyone named Ivy Srutwa.

CHAPTER 46

In the early afternoon Ivy parked her car on a side street and walked briskly towards the hospital. Frank had confirmed that Wim was a doctor, so it must be the same guy. Chances were slim that there would be two doctors named Wim Winston.

He was the only one remaining of Ivy's tormentors. The others had been taken care of and that made her man task so much easier. She said a silent prayer of thanks to whomever it was that had helped her by killing Dwight, jailing Duane, and turning Ronnie Fowler into the eighteenth fattest man in the world.

She bargained on Wim not remembering her.

The hospital part was fun. Ivy liked the hospital. She thought she'd like to work in one in some capacity. Maybe she could volunteer. The museum had always been her thing, the thing she did for Simon, for the eyes of the world—it was part of earning her keep. And it wasn't hard. But maybe she could change to a hospital. Surely that would seem more worthwhile, more giving. She could take flowers to patients, wash their hair, wheel around the library cart.

They could tell me their stories, she thought. Maybe one of them would like me.

But the Nelson Mac reunion was taking up her time right now. She was really into it. It was her current for-the-eyes-of-the-world project. It was what had come to her when she went to see Frank. She amazed herself. Didn't even know that she knew about it. She supposed it had been mentioned in tiny print in the Community Review section of the *Free Press*. And for some reason—which now was clear—it had lodged itself in her brain. It was a perfect way to get close to Frank. Not that she fully understood why that was necessary. It just was.

Ivy knew he didn't trust her. But that didn't matter. She liked knowing him, being around him. She had to think up more reasons that would let it happen. Maybe after she pulled everything off she could be his friend. In her heart she knew she couldn't, but she couldn't find her heart.

The cafeteria was on the second floor of the hospital. Ivy sipped coffee and watched people come and go—doctors, nurses, orderlies, aides, physiotherapists, cleaners, administrative types, visitors, patients. She listed different occupations in her notebook and put numbers beneath them as the cafeteria filled up with the Friday lunch crowd. Then she stopped herself. I'm never going to be able to get anything done on either my own projects or the for-the-eyes-of-the-world projects if I can't stop this type of thing. She put her pencil and paper away.

Her hands began to shake and her eye twitched as she sat alone at her table trying not to make lists. Someone sat too close and she spilled her coffee. Not on herself, thank God. She couldn't have stood that.

The optimism Ivy had felt when she entered the hospital was gone and she could barely focus on putting one high-heeled shoe in front of the other as she stumbled out of the cafeteria.

If she had been able to concentrate on anything but the Squeaks nattering in her brain, she might have noticed the name tag on the doctor jammed up against her in the crowded elevator.

It read: Dr. Wim Winston.

"What a babe," Wim said to his colleague when Ivy got off at street level with most of the other passengers. "I coulda stayed squashed up against that ass indefinitely."

When the Squeaks stopped, Ivy was sitting on a bench on the main floor of the hospital holding a hammer with a rough wooden handle. When she saw it clutched in her hands she stuffed it inside her handbag with some difficulty.

She closed her eyes and breathed deeply till her heart stopped pounding and her vision cleared. She needed a drink of water.

The bench where she sat was across the hall from a snack bar. The snacks were in machines. Ivy fumbled in her purse for change but couldn't come up with the right combination. She was so thirsty!

The tables were all empty. She pictured herself ploughing her fist through the front of the machine and snatching up the Evian Water that smirked up at her from its prison of metal and glass. Instead she took her lipstick from her makeup pouch and wrote, SCRUNT, in big red letters on one of the smooth table surfaces.

It wasn't enough. But something caught her eye and her anger vanished along with her thirst. On the wall next to the door was a bulletin board. And on the bulletin board was a notice. GOLF TOURNAMENT! it said, followed by the particulars.

The place was a club on the east side of the city where Ivy had played before, when Simon was fit and they had done things together. Simon had known someone who was a member there who'd had them as guests.

The date was a Saturday, two weeks away. Two weeks and one day. The tournament was open to all hospital personnel and the contact person was Dr. Wim Winston.

CHAPTER 47

Frank sat at his desk with his feet resting on a pulled-out drawer. He didn't have Ivy's number. He didn't even know her husband's first name. Setting his knitting aside he looked Grace up in the phone book. She was obviously well-to-do. Maybe her husband was the Grace in Grace, Royston & Wells. If he was, he was old, unless he had a son that Ivy had glommed onto. It wouldn't surprise Frank if her husband turned out to be elderly. It would go with the rest of the picture.

There weren't very many Graces. Frank had just dialed the number of the first one when there was a knock on his door. He sighed and hung up the phone.

It was Fred. He came in and closed the door behind him. He stood at attention in front of the desk but there was a sag to his shoulders that Frank hadn't seen before. And his top button was undone; that was definitely a first.

"What is it, Fred?" Frank asked. "Is everything okay?"

"Thanks, sir. No, everything isn't okay. But I don't feel as though I can talk about it. Not right now, anyway." He looked over Frank's shoulder when he spoke.

Frank looked carefully to his right just in case there was something to see. Nope.

"Okay, Fred. But you can talk to me anytime. I hope you know that. It sometimes helps, you know, to get it off your chest."

I should know, thought Frank, who felt several degrees lighter after having shared his own tale of woe with Ed Flagston. In spite of everything he had yet to do.

He was pretty sure there were tears in Fred's eyes. What was he doing here if he didn't want to talk?

"Nothing will be able to help in this case, sir," Fred said. "It's done and it can't be undone."

"But still, it might help to talk." Frank realized that he hadn't hidden his wool. It sat on top of his desk next to the open phone book.

"No," Fred said. "I don't think so, sir."

Frank wondered if he swatted Fred on the side of the head at the exact moment that he told him not to call him "sir", if that might work.

"It's Frances, sir."

"What about her, Fred?"

"She doesn't want to have a baby."

"Oh?" He placed Emma's scarf gently in its drawer.

"Ever."

"Well, lots of couples live quite happily without children," Frank said. He immediately regretted encouraging Fred to confide in him. This could have been Frank fifteen years ago.

"Yeah, I guess," Fred said.

Frank tried to think up something smart to say. He closed the phone book and rearranged the items on his desk. There weren't very many of them.

"She had an abortion," Fred said.

"Oh?" Frank moved his paperweight so that it faced Fred. It was a duck. Sadie had given it to him for his birthday.

"She did it without telling me," Fred said.

"Oh." Frank remembered how he had lain awake nights worrying that Denise would do just that.

"We hadn't planned the baby," Fred said, "but I had thought we were happy about it. I know I was."

"It sounds like there may have been a bit of a communication breakdown somewhere along the way," Frank said.

"I can't believe she did it without telling me she was going to."

"Maybe she was afraid you'd try and talk her out of it."

"I would have."

"Yes."

"It's not natural for a young woman to not want to have a baby, is it, sir? It seems crazy to me."

"She may have all kinds of reasons, Fred, or one very good one, anyway. You've got to talk to each other." Frank turned the duck back around so it was facing him.

"She won't talk, sir."

"Then go home and put your arms around her, Fred."

"My shift isn't over."

"Go home, Fred."

"I'm a fine one to be giving marital advice," Frank said to his paperweight after Fred had gone. He opened the phone book and then closed it again. He knew he wouldn't find Ivy that way. He hummed an old Beatles' song from 1965 as he hauled the scarf out of his drawer to resume work. Frank was considering knitting lessons if there was such a thing. Not knowing how to make anything but scarves was pitiful and he felt he should be progressing with his hobby. But scarves were so easy. There was no need to worry about sleeves or collars or buttons or anything—sheer pleasure.

"I'm a loser," he sang, "and I'm not what I appear to be."

His phone rang and he picked it up.

"Foote," he said.

"Frank?"

"Yes."

It was Ivy Grace.

CHAPTER 48

Emma jerked awake and sat bolt upright in her bed. The clock radio was invisible. Lightning pierced the sky outside her bedroom window and she realized it must have been the thunder that woke her. The power had gone out and screwed up her clock. She would have to reset it—she couldn't be late for her papers.

Her bedside light wouldn't turn on. So the power hadn't come back—she would have to wait it out. She would never get back to sleep if her alarm wasn't set.

Emma crept over to the window seat to keep an eye on the storm. Rain had poured through the open window, so she pushed it closed and tossed the soaked cushions onto the floor. In the yard the wind and rain lashed against the cedar trees, bending them sideways. Emma watched as it began to let up. Lightning flashed again and lit the yard as clear as day. A tall figure leaned against the garage beneath the carport, sheltered from the weather.

Emma gasped and darted back behind her curtain. The woman had been looking at her this time. Emma saw her eyes in the flash of light.

In the dark again, she peered around the curtain and saw the burning end of a cigarette glowing through the wet night. She crawled across the floor to the bedroom door and ran down the hall to her dad's room. The door was ajar and he lay awake.

"Dad?" she whispered.

"Yes, Em dear, what is it?" He turned on his light and the room flooded with warmth.

"Oh, Dad, there's someone in the yard." As she spoke she doubted her own words and wondered if it might have been a dream. Her dad's lamp worked. The power was on!

"Who?" Frank asked. "Who's in the yard?"

"I don't know. A tall person. I saw her in the lightning. She was looking up at me."

"Her? She?" Frank's brow furrowed. His furrows no longer went away when he relaxed, but sometimes they went deeper than other times, like now.

Emma moved to the bed and into his arms. "It was really scary, Dad." She started to cry against his blue pajama top.

Frank hugged his daughter tight. He loved her so much his heart hurt. "Let's go have a look."

They walked back down the hall to her room holding hands. Emma wouldn't go in.

"She was over by the garage, underneath the carport."

Frank peered out at the dark yard. "What did she look like?" The rain had stopped and the wind had died so he opened the window.

"I don't know. Tall? Womanly?"

Water dripped, but other than that nothing stirred.

"I don't think anyone's there, Em." Frank noticed the alarm clock flashing. "I guess the power was out."

"Yeah. I've gotta reset my alarm." Emma edged her way into the room. "Dad, I don't wanna do my papers in the morning."

"Oh, honey, tomorrow's a new day." Frank closed the window and locked it. "What say we go downstairs and have a look around outside to put our minds at rest?"

They tucked their pajama bottoms into rubber boots and tramped around the yard, front and back. In the carport Emma thought she could smell cigarette smoke, but Frank couldn't.

Gus was on his back stoop whispering at them when they headed back to the house.

"I don't know what the heck you two are up to out there, but I never sleep after a thunderstorm so I decided to make some cocoa. Want some?"

Frank and Emma laughed. Gus' noisy whispering was something of a family joke. They played Crazy Eights till dawn. Then Frank took Emma home and made her waffles for breakfast. After that he accompanied her to her paper pick-up spot.

Twice. Both times in the rain. Both times in the dark. Frank hadn't prayed since he was a kid but he prayed now: Don't let anything bad happen to Emma. Ever. Please.

They delivered papers in the tranquil morning. So far, the doves were their only companions.

"Pretty day, eh, Em?" Frank said. He saw Easy and his master run by on Lyndale Drive at the top of the street.

"Yeah, pretty," she said. "But scary."

There wasn't a cloud in the sky. It was hot already and the air was thick with last night's rain. It was one of those late spring days where you could almost see the leaves growing before your eyes.

There were no sinister automobiles or shadowy staring figures. But they weren't far from the imaginations of either Foote as they went on their rounds. Frank was painfully aware that he wouldn't always be able to be there, watching over his daughter.

It was so calm. Even the mourning doves were quiet now. The only sound was the hum of the city across the river, whatever combination of electricity, physics and chemistry produced that one sound that never went away. The soundtrack to their lives.

Frank thought about the first time he had used his computer at work, when he realized it was going to be humming quietly the whole time it was turned on. He was furious. When he mentioned it, nobody seemed to know what he was talking about. It was such an unobtrusive sound, the way everyone else heard it. Why would it bother him? So he decided not to let it. He hadn't wanted to stand out as someone who couldn't handle things like quiet sounds.

Sometimes he thought that all the new noises—invented after WW II, as Gus would point out—were the main cause of everything gone wrong in people's heads. It was the racket that drove them crazy. This was the type of thing he saved to talk to Gus about; Gus got things like that. What a good neighbour he was!

Easy and his master jogged up behind them and stopped.

"Good morning, Emma, Frank," the man said.

"Good morning," they answered.

"You'll have to forgive me," Frank said. "I can't remember your name."

"Rupe," Emma and the man said together.

Rupe smiled and Frank smiled back.

Emma tussled with Easy on the boulevard.

"Could I talk to you for a minute, Frank?" Rupe wiped his brow on a small towel he carried fastened to his shorts—a real professional.

"Of course." Frank eyed Rupe's waistband, the flat stomach underneath the tucked in T-shirt. He touched his own gut, which protruded gently over the top of his jeans.

"Emma, I'm going to talk to Rupe for a minute. You go on ahead and I'll catch up."

"Okay. Can Easy come with me?" she asked Rupe.

"Of course he can," he said. "Go with Emma, Ease. I'll be right along."

"Come on, boy," Emma said.

The dog trotted off with Emma, who pulled her wagon behind her.

The two men stood awkwardly in the middle of the road for a few moments till Rupe finally spoke.

"You may think I'm way out of line here, but I feel I have to say something to you."

"What is it, Rupe?"

"It's that woman I saw you with at The Forks the other day."

"Mmm-hmm?"

Obviously Rupe had the wrong idea about what he was doing with Ivy, but Frank wanted to hear what the man had to say before he got into making excuses for himself. He wondered why he didn't think Rupe was being a "buttinsky", as Gus would say. He sensed the kindness in the man. Rupe wasn't enjoying this—he wanted to help.

"She's bad news, Frank. I had a one-nighter, or I should say a one-morninger with her a couple of years ago and...well...I just feel as though it was a terrible mistake."

"What do you mean, Rupe?"

"Well...the reason I hesitated to say anything is that it's more just a feeling I have about her than anything else. A feeling that she's not quite right somehow."

Frank watched Emma as she turned the corner at the end of the street and suddenly he didn't want her out of his sight. Easy had stopped and stationed himself so that he could keep an eye on both Emma and his master.

"Why don't we talk while we walk?" Frank smiled. "I don't want to get too far behind or I may never catch up."

Rupe looked miserable as he fell in beside Frank. "That's about it, really," he said. "She seems dangerous to me. I felt afterwards like I should have run from her."

"I haven't had sex with her." Frank felt fifteen years old.

"Good!" Rupe said. "It's not my business what your connection is to her. God, I don't even know her name. She wouldn't tell me. But I just wanted to…well…warn you, I guess. She's not a regular-type person. I think she's sick or evil or something. I'm sorry, Frank."

"No, no, don't worry, Rupe." Frank liked this man. "I appreciate the information." He used his policeman's voice as a substitute for any more words of denial which he knew would ring false. Odd as Ivy was, and far-fetched as the idea of sleeping with her was, he couldn't deny he'd pictured it and been more than a little curious.

Except for the fact that she probably had AIDS. If she was indeed little Jane Doe's mother, which Frank was becoming more and more convinced that she was. If only it didn't take so ridiculously long for DNA test results to come back. And he didn't even have a sample yet! He would see her today and get something if he had to squeeze it out of her himself.

"Were you tested for the HIV virus?" he asked Rupe.

"Yeah. It came back negative, thank God. This was quite a while ago and I got tested again recently, so I'm sure I'm in the clear."

Rupe began interspersing the odd jog in with his walking steps which indicated to Frank that the conversation was over.

"All right then, Rupe. Thanks again. We'll see ya."

"Okay, Frank. And again, I'm sorry to butt in."

"Don't worry."

"Okay. See you then."

Rupe darted down the street after Easy and Emma, and Frank also broke into a run till he had his daughter in clear view.

So Ivy was into anonymous sex. Somehow, Frank wasn't surprised by this information. He felt as though he had been expecting it. Especially after the way Rupe and Ivy had reacted to seeing each other. It was obvious something had been going on there.

"What did he want to talk about?" Emma asked, when he had caught up.

"Oh nothing much, really." Frank gasped for breath. "He knows I'm a cop, so he wanted to ask me some noise by-law questions. He has a neighbour who's on his case about Easy barking."

"Easy doesn't bark."

"Well, maybe it was something else the neighbour was on about. I wasn't listening very carefully."

"Honestly, Dad, you should pay attention when people talk to you. You didn't even remember Rupe's name. You might miss something important some day."

"You're right. Sorry. Now let's get these papers delivered before we start getting hollered at."

"Dad?"

"Yes?"

"Were you running?"

"Yeah, maybe a little." Frank was still puffing a bit.

"I don't think I've ever seen you run before. What's the story?"

"No story, Em. I guess maybe Rupe got me thinking about how out of shape I am." Among other things, Frank thought.

"Well," Emma said. "Don't hurt yourself. You can't just start running, you know, just like that. Not at your age and not with stupid shoes on."

Frank looked down at his fifteen-year-old boat shoes and laughed.

"You're right, Emma," he said. "Where would I be without you to order me around?"

Much as he hated the idea, Frank decided to phone Wim again and try to warn him against Ivy.

CHAPTER 49

Ivy had phoned Frank to ask him about his progress with the list she had left with him. He made a date with her to get together for a drink. He hadn't spent any time trying to track down any more of the names on the list, but the Nelson Mac reunion was ostensibly his reason for seeing her, so he closed the door to his office now and got busy.

It was late Saturday afternoon. It seemed like he never took a whole day off anymore.

There were sixteen people on the list unaccounted for. He figured that if he could find two of them it would be enough.

Frank had supper with his kids—barbecued hamburgers, a veggie burger for Emma. Then he went to the hospital to visit Denise. He almost told her about Ivy and then didn't.

Denise asked about the kids, seemed genuinely interested, so Frank told her an anecdote about Sadie: He and Sadie had been sitting side by side on the couch watching a rerun of *The Simpsons*. Frank hadn't been paying strict attention. He'd been thinking about Ivy Grace—but he didn't mention that part to Denise.

"Jesus Christ," Sadie had said.

"What!" Frank gaped at his daughter.

"I was just sayin' 'Jesus Christ of the Latter Day Saints.'" Sadie smiled up at him.

Frank looked at the TV in time to catch the last of a commercial for that particular brand of religion.

"Well, I can hardly holler at you for that, can I?" He had laughed and given Sadie a hug. "Yup, that's quite a mouthful."

Denise smiled as Frank told the story. "I miss them, Frank," she said. "I miss tucking them in and kissing them goodnight."

"They miss you too," he said.

At 8:45 he pulled into the parking lot of the Tap and Grill on Osborne Street and went inside to meet Ivy.

The evening had turned cool after the heat of the day. The weather was so changeable. Frank wondered if it was just regular changeableness or part of some huge phenomenon like El Niño or La Niña or the end of the world.

Ivy wore a cream-coloured cardigan over her summer dress. Her jet black hair brushed her shoulders. Frank didn't think Caucasians had hair as black as that. It had to be dyed.

They ordered drinks—Frank a beer and Ivy a mineral water. Damn! It would be easier to snatch her glass out from under her if she was feeling a little tipsy. Why couldn't she have ordered a stinger!

Frank eyed her handbag. For sure there would be a lipstick in there. But he doubted he would have a chance to rifle through it. If she went to the washroom, she would take it with her. That's the reason women visited washrooms, to haul stuff out of their purses and use it on themselves.

Ivy opened her handbag, reached in and pulled out a new pack of Matinee cigarettes. She smoked. This was going to be easier than he thought.

"Ivy! I didn't know you smoked. I don't think you did the last time we got together."

She smiled and lit one with a match from Hy's Steak Loft. "Just sometimes. I hope it doesn't bother you."

"Not at all!"

She smoked it half-way down to the filter and put it out. Frank hoped that the waitress wouldn't be too keen about cleaning the ashtray the way they were in some places.

Ivy took her sweater off and hung it over the back of her chair. He was pretty sure he could see a hair attached to it. The bar was dimly lit though. He couldn't be certain.

"Excuse me, Frank. I have to use the ladies' room," she said and picked up her purse.

"Certainly, Ivy." Frank found himself partially standing up to see her off. What was that all about? He had never done that before in his life.

She was gone. Clear out of the room. Carefully, Frank picked the cigarette butt out of the ashtray, placed it in a plastic evidence bag, sealed it, and put it in his pocket. Then he stood up and looked closely at her sweater. Sure enough, there was a hair, complete with follicle. He removed it and placed it on a white napkin on the table. He fumbled in his pocket for another bag and ever so gently he placed the hair inside, sealed it and returned it to his pocket alongside the cigarette butt. There was a button on that particular pocket so he fastened it. Frank waved the waitress over and asked her for a clean ashtray.

Ed Flagston would be expecting the samples Monday morning. He had set the wheels in motion, completed the paperwork and even spoken to his brother-in-law on the phone. The wife's brother had said he would do his best to rush the job, but he had made no promises.

The waitress returned with a clean ashtray at the same time that Ivy came back from the washroom.

"Thank you." Ivy smiled at her.

Frank gave Ivy his list of two names for the reunion.

She laughed. "I see this hasn't really been a priority for you, Frank."

He smiled. "Well, things have been kind of busy for me lately. Sorry."

"It's okay. It's nice to see you anyway." She reached out to touch his hand.

Frank jumped as though her touch was fire.

CHAPTER 50

It was after eleven when Frank got home. The two younger kids were in bed. Emma should be in bed too, Frank thought, when he heard voices coming from the rec room. That damn television.

Sometimes he could almost find himself agreeing with Gus that practically nothing worthwhile had been invented since the second world war. What were Gus' exceptions? Car turning signals, dental floss, and in-line roller skates, of all things. Gus admired in-line skates and wondered why it had taken them so long to be invented. He wished they had been around in his youth.

Frank chuckled to himself as he remembered Gus' explanation of why he wouldn't own a pair of skates now. It turned out he was scared to try them in case he fell down and broke both his arms or hands and had to hire someone to wipe his ass. An understandable fear.

The rec room was dark except for the flickering of the tube.

"Hi, Dad," Emma said.

"Hi, Em." Frank turned on a lamp. "Hi, Donald."

"Hi, Mr. Foote."

"What are you two up to?"

Please don't have been necking, Frank thought. I'm not ready for that yet. He thought back to his own teen years when he used to join Audrey at her baby-sitting jobs, and remembered that it had always been done secretively because the parents of her charges frowned upon it. They had been caught once, caught big. They weren't exactly doing it, but may as well have been, considering the state of their clothes—they wore none—and their obliviousness to what was going on around them. Mr. Wheatley actually had to say, 'Ahem!' before they realized he was there. Mrs. Wheatley was nowhere to be seen. They guessed the situation proved too much for her. Audrey hadn't been asked back to baby-sit there or anywhere else; word had gotten around.

Emma and Donald didn't look as though they'd been necking.

"We're just watching a movie about a volcano," Emma said. "We thought it might help us with my science project. I guess you could say we're doing homework."

Frank laughed. "Well, I hope it's almost over. It's getting pretty late. Does your mum know you're here, Donald?"

"Yup."

Frank sat.

The kids that aren't criminals seem so sensible nowadays, he thought. The ones I know anyway. I don't know very many. But they're way more sensible than we ever were.

"Can I give you a lift home, Donald?" he asked.

"Thanks, Mr. Foote, but I've got my bike."

The credits started to roll and Emma pressed the rewind button.

"So how's the volcano project coming, anyway?" Frank asked.

"We're just gathering information at this stage," Donald said. "Laying the groundwork."

Frank was pretty sure he liked Donald. The kid talked, which was good. And he wore glasses, which also seemed good to Frank, although he didn't know why.

He just didn't want him touching his daughter.

"I think it'll end up being really great," Donald added and smiled at Emma, who smiled back.

"I can drop the tape off on my way home," he said, getting up.

"Okay." Emma stood up and stretched. "I'll walk you to your bike."

"Goodnight, Mr. Foote."

"Goodnight, Donald."

Frank wondered if they were kissing at the door. But Emma came back almost immediately.

"You like Donald, eh Em?"

"Yeah, I do, Dad."

"He seems very fond of you too."

"Do you think so? I think so and then I don't and then I do again. It's confusing."

Frank grinned at his daughter and wished that Denise was here to offer some kind of female perspective on this new situation in Emma's life. What the hell did he know? And then he remembered that Emma had said that she hated her mother.

"Seeing him makes me feel kind of funny inside. But a good kind of funny," she said. "Know what I mean?"

"Yeah, Em. I think I know pretty much exactly what you mean."

"Well, I think I'll call it a day." Emma yawned.

"I'm just going to stay here and fool around with my new wool for a while before bed." Frank opened a drawer in the table beside his easy chair.

"Goodnight, Dad." Emma smiled.

"Goodnight, Em."

Frank hauled out a deep green ball of wool and laid it next to a beige one. Maybe a sweater for Sadie. There was a series of knitting workshops being offered at the high school and Frank had made inquiries. The participants were supposed to have decided on a project before the first class and to have purchased the wool and a pattern. Nothing too complicated, but not too simple either, the woman had said on the phone. Like, no scarves. Well, he had the wool.

Maybe tomorrow I'll scout around for a pattern, Frank thought, as he turned out the lights and headed up to bed.

CHAPTER 51

It wasn't hard for Ivy to get a membership at the golf club. Being married to Simon Grace was still a good thing in many respects. Grace, Royston & Wells was still one of the most highly regarded law firms in the city, even though all three original partners were long out of it.

She joined the club as Tara. Tara Grace.

Ivy had enjoyed golfing once—she had been good at it. She knew there was no hope of getting through nine holes these days with her concentration problems. But there was nothing stopping her from hanging out in the restaurant and bar. She could make a day of it on the Saturday of the tournament. And she would take care to look her very best.

It turned out that the best thing about joining the club was the swimming. Tara Grace swam and swam. In the crystal blue water she was free. And transparent, like the wings of a dragon fly. The muck that filled her head and body disappeared in the water and she longed to feel that way forever.

The outdoor pool was the best. Lying on her back, she stared up at the fresh green leaves against the late spring sky and would have died there if given the choice. It was early in the season, so often she would have the pool all to herself. The air was sometimes cool but the water was always warm.

She couldn't stay in the pool forever, but it came to her that when the confusion occurred, the interruptions that sent her off in different directions, she could come here and let it all float away. When her timing was right, she would find herself alone in the water, knowing she was exactly where she was supposed to be.

It was in the pool on the last day of May, a half week before the day of the golf tournament that Tara was finally able to divide and categorize the three voices in her head.

She wrote these concepts down in her notebook when she got out of the pool. They were sharp-edged and clear. She loved the clarity more than anything.

CHAPTER 52

On Friday, the day before the tournament, Tara had another perfect swim. No one but her—that was essential.

By the end of it, she saw her plans laid out neatly and completely in front of her. It was as though they had always been there. She just had to sweep away the dust gently, like dusting for fingerprints, to reveal the true deal. True deals: there were three of them and they sparkled and shone before her.

Tara laughed out loud as she climbed the steps out of the pool and dried her hands and face on a towel so thick she couldn't dry the insides of her ears.

She stretched out on a lawn chair and retrieved her notebook from her bag. She knew what each voice wanted and on a brand new page she wrote: Ivy's Three Tasks. Beneath the heading she listed them in point form.

And then she closed her eyes and went to sleep.

And in spite of her afternoon nap, Ivy slept soundly on Friday night. Nothing worried her.

She breakfasted with her husband early on Saturday morning.

"Simon, I was wondering if we could get a swimming pool built in our backyard."

Simon was still reeling from the sight of his wife across the dining table from him. It had been weeks, maybe months, since she had joined him for breakfast. He peered at her as closely as he dared.

"You look different, my dear. What is it that's changed?"

Ivy laughed. "You probably haven't seen me without makeup for a very long time. Maybe that's it."

Simon realized that she was right. She looked pretty in the sunlight shining through the window. A soft pretty—a little taut maybe—but not the hard scary gorgeous that he had grown used to.

"You look nice," he said and to his chagrin felt a tear escape and slide into one of the vertical crevices in his face.

"What do you think?" Ivy asked. "The yard's big enough."

She lit a cigarette. "I've found that I really like swimming."

"I don't see why not," said Simon.

Although he dreaded the construction noise and workmen stomping about, it seemed like a good, healthy idea to him, one that should be encouraged.

"Okay, great." She pressed her cool lips against his forehead. "I've gotta run. I'm going to watch a golf tournament today."

"A what?"

"A golf tournament. At the Prairie Hills. I'm a member there now. I swim mostly, but it's starting to get crowded now the weather's warming up. That's why I'd like a pool here at home."

Ivy went off to get ready for the day and Simon spoke to his dog.

"She's a puzzler, Lucy girl. She puzzles the heck out of me. What do you think?"

Lucy whapped her tail on the floor and rested her grizzled snout between her two front paws. Simon reached down to stroke her head and realized he felt better than he had in days.

"How would you like to go for a walk today, Lucy?"

It had been a long time since Simon had been out with his dog. Sometimes Lena was kind enough to take her for a modest romp in the park but nothing like what Lucy had been used to before Simon got sick. She sat up at the word walk, not excited yet but prepared for excitement if what she thought was happening should turn out to be true.

Simon chuckled and called out, "Lena, let's you and me and Lucy take a stroll."

Ivy prepared herself like a school girl going on a first date with a boy she loved. Except for the cuts. A school girl wouldn't slice into the tender flesh of her most secret self to ensure that her tainted blood would flow easily.

She bathed and showered till she shone and took extra care with her hair and makeup. There would be no swim today. She had to look perfect. The outfit she chose emphasized the curves of her body and her long shapely legs without seeming to do so on purpose: a crimson silk shirt that fell gently against the black lace covering the smooth skin of her breasts; a straight black skirt, also silk, long enough to look right on someone her age, but short enough to rise well above her knees when seated; and delicate Italian sandals with four-inch heels. Ivy admired the way she looked in high-heeled shoes and she had no intention of traipsing around the golf course. She was sure she could manage just fine from inside the clubhouse and patio areas.

Tara Grace was a good new name. Ivy was glad she had chosen it and pleased with herself for taking out her membership under that name. She knew Wim wouldn't know her. Why would he? Frank hadn't recognized her and he was more the type who would. He looked at people.

Maybe she would keep the name Tara even after she was done here. Ivy could disappear.

It was easy. Wim Winston was easy.

"Don't I know you?" he said as he sidled up to her at the bar.

"No, I'm sure you don't." She pushed away the image of him panting over her in the penalty box and with it the shame that covered her like a steamy blanket.

Wim laughed. "Yes, I do. Don't tell me what I do or don't know!"

He's still an asshole, Tara thought. "Whatever." She turned back to her mineral water and took a sip. If he knew she was Ivy Srutwa, chances were good he wouldn't want to fuck her. She hadn't bargained on this.

"I've seen you before. I know I have," Wim said. "I've got it. It was at the hospital a while back, the hospital where I work. I'd never forget someone as beautiful as you."

Tara sat up straight and smiled a slow smile. "Well, thank you."

"May I buy you another drink?" he asked.

"No, thanks," Tara said. "But you can tell me your name."

"Wim."

She laughed. "I know that from your name tag, I mean your last name, Wim."

"Winston. Dr. Winston," he added and she laughed again.

"A pleasure to meet you, Dr. Winston. Perhaps we'll meet again." She stood to go.

"Wait! Don't go! Are you a member here? Do you come here often?"

Ivy backed her Triumph out of the parking lot. That was enough for today. It couldn't have gone better, she thought. Except for the scare when he said he knew me. But that passed soon enough.

She drove the Triumph only on certain occasions, left the Lincoln in the garage and went for a sportier look. The top was down on the little red car and Ivy hummed along with the radio. The days ahead looked tidy and clean. Everything in its place.

CHAPTER 53

Denise was being released soon to a room in a house for recovering addicts. She was neither glad nor sad. At least she wouldn't have to worry about running into Wim at the hospital anymore. He had stopped coming to see her a couple of weeks before, but she didn't feel safe from him, knowing that he could appear at any time, breezing into the ward with his doctor's badge.

She pulled the curtain around and lay down on her bed to wait for her husband to come by.

Frank hung up his phone and sighed. This time when he called, he knew that the secretary was lying because he could hear Wim in the background. "If it's Frank Foote, tell him I'm not here," he said. "If it's Frank Foote, tell him I'm gone."

Okay, Wim. You win.

It was time to visit Denise.

CHAPTER 54

Wim Winston was a prick.

He wanted to fuck her by the river and in the back of his car and in the washroom at the golf club. Tara had seen him with his wife at dinner in the restaurant and she pitied the woman who shared her life with such a loathsome man. She knew there was a chance she would be killing the wife as well, but she couldn't think too much about that. And anyway, what was so terrible about death?

Ivy approved of Wim's taste in places. Blood mixed better with grass and old blankets than it did with crisp hotel sheets.

But she didn't want to have to do this for much longer. It was odious work. It wasn't that Wim was a lousy fuck, as fucks went. But she hated every single thing about him. There was nothing that she didn't hate. She would rather have fucked a mean dog.

She didn't want to have to kiss him anymore. If he could just do her it wouldn't be so bad. But he wanted to smooch and cuddle and talk and she didn't think she could stomach one more night of that.

Ivy yanked out one of her back teeth. She used pliers and it took forever. The tooth broke and there was a horrible mess in her mouth by the time she held the roots in her hand. She grinned at her bloody face in the mirror over her bathroom sink.

"You taste like blood," Wim said.

It was late Friday night and they lay on a blanket behind the pavilion in City Park.

She hated the way he kissed her mouth while he fucked her. He opened his own mouth so wide he got her face all wet. And his tongue was pointed, like a snake's head; it darted about leaving no corner unsullied. She was so glad it was over. Wim Winston was dead.

"I pulled a tooth today," she said.

"What?" Wim stopped.

"I had a tooth pulled today." She changed the words to suit him.

"I can't get enough of you, Tara," he said, and buried his face in her hair. "You're killing me."

Ivy smiled. If he only knew. "I won't be able to see you after tonight," she said.

"What!"

"I can't see you anymore, Wim." Ivy lit a cigarette, lay back and gazed at the sliver of a moon.

"What are you talking about? You can't not see me anymore!"

"Yes, I can't." She giggled. A silvery new moon sound. "Go away now, Wim. I can walk home from here."

Ivy lay naked and beautiful in the starlight and Wim hounded her while she laughed at him. He begged for an explanation but she didn't think he deserved one. When he slapped her face she howled. He struggled with his shoes and finally ran off half clothed towards Park Boulevard where he had left his car.

Ivy watched the dark night enshroud his pale form before he reached the street. It would be easy never to lay eyes on him again. She would just quit the club.

CHAPTER 55

Emma and Donald were baby-sitting Garth and Sadie. They still hadn't kissed and Emma thought about it all the time. There was no way she was going to be the one to start it. But she would be ready when it finally happened.

They built a mountain, smoothing the papier mâché into shape, adding water to keep it workable till it looked just right. They leaned over the volcano from opposite sides of the kitchen table, meeting in the middle. Emma worked at forming the opening at the top, where they hoped their dry ice and baking powder mixture would do its job of simulating an eruption. They were going to light it up from the inside with a couple of reddish-orange Christmas lights to give it a fiery glow. An unsteady light—Donald was working on that.

He had spoken to a friend of his, Leonard, who was an ice-cream man, about getting a slab of dry ice. And he had a book called *Let's Experiment* which he had brought with him tonight. They planned to pore over it later to see if it contained any tips on modest explosions.

Donald started to kiss her for the first time, on the lips, there over the volcano. At the precise moment that his lips touched hers a scream echoed wildly through the house from the direction of Garth's bedroom. Emma and Donald raced up the stairs to find a terrified Garth on the floor beside his bed. His small body quivered and Emma held him in her mucky papier mâché arms.

"Shh, little guy. It was just a bad dream."

"I dreamed I was buried alive," Garth whispered.

"Oh, Garth." Emma kissed his damp forehead. "That's what comes from watching those scary movies."

He'd had a friend over to sleep the night before, and Emma had heard them sneak downstairs in the middle of the night and then the television sounds.

"You're all wet," Garth said.

"We're working on the volcano."

"What movie did you watch?" Donald asked.

"*Premature Burial.*"

"Oh boy. I saw that one too. It scared the hell out of me. 'Specially that scene when they dug the guy up. No wonder you were frightened right out of your bed. I'm surprised you weren't propelled clear out the window."

Garth smiled a little. "Yeah, that was the part that scared me too."

"Do you wanna come down and help us build the volcano for a while?" Emma asked. "We could make some cocoa."

"Yes, please."

When Emma bundled Garth into his little maroon robe and slippers she noticed that he was wearing two watches.

"What's with the watches, Garth?"

"Well…if I wear two, I'll still know what time it is when one of them stops…while I get a new battery. And then I can be sure the new battery will tide me over when the other watch stops. It's foolproof. Unless a huge rock falls on my wrist or something."

"Sounds complicated," Emma said.

"Not really." Garth checked his wrist and then his alarm clock.

"Why do you wear them to bed?" Donald asked.

"It saves putting them on in the morning. Also, if there's a fire in the night and we have to escape and leave everything behind, I'll at least have my watches and know what time it is."

"Whew!" Emma hoped Donald didn't think Garth was too weird. She carried her brother down the stairs piggyback, stopping first to check on Sadie, who was sound asleep.

"Amazing," Emma said.

When they were settled around the volcano, with their cocoa and marshmallows, Garth said, "I don't want anybody to die."

Emma looked at Donald and he looked back at her. Garth watched them look at each other.

"No one's gonna die," Emma said.

"Yes they are. Mum and Dad are gonna die because they're way older than us."

"Well, someday, yeah. But not for a long, long, long, long time. Not until you've been a grownup yourself for many, many years. And by that time you'll get that it's okay."

"No, I won't," Garth said.

Emma didn't argue.

"My dad died," Donald said. "He was in a car accident a few years ago."

Emma and Garth stared at him.

"The way I got to finally thinking about it is that if a great guy like my dad died, it must be okay to die."

"My dad's great too," Garth said.

"I'm sorry about your dad, Donald," Emma said. "I figured your parents were probably divorced or something."

"It's okay. I'm really okay with it. I mean, I miss him and all, but…"

"Do you think guys get buried alive very often?" Garth asked.

The back door slammed.

"I'll bury you alive in a minute!"

"Dad!" Garth zoomed into his father's arms.

"Garth's a little freaked out from watching *Premature Burial*," Emma said.

"Oh he is, is he? And what's he doing watching something like that? Hi, Donald."

"Hi, Mr. Foote."

"Him and Gilbert watched it last night in secret," Emma said. "Do you want some cocoa, Dad? There's lots."

"Well, maybe just this once, Em. Just half a cup." Frank sat down with Garth on his knee.

"You'd think the way I sleep I'd wake up long enough to holler at my boy in the middle of the night when he's doing something stupid. Wow! Look at your volcano! It looks wonderful!"

"Yeah," Emma said. "It's comin' along."

Frank smoothed the hair back off Garth's forehead. "The answer to your buried alive question is no. People never get buried alive."

Emma placed a steaming mug of cocoa on the table in front of her dad.

"Thanks, Em." He gently nudged Garth off his knee. "The folks who get the bodies ready for burial, the undertakers they call them, make one hundred per cent certain that people are dead forever before they put them in their coffins."

"What if there's an evil undertaker?" Garth asked.

"He's really freaked," Emma explained.

"Well, something else you can do is be cremated." Frank sipped his drink. "Mmm. This is great."

"What's that?" Garth asked. "What's cremated?"

"Well, the body gets burned in a big fire so that nothing is left but ashes. Kind of an enclosed bonfire. No one watches or anything."

"Hmm," Garth said.

"That sounds good to me," Donald said. "Sign me up."

"Yeah, that does sound good," Garth said. "How do you let people know that's what you want to have happen to you?"

"Well, most folks make their wishes known before they die. To their loved ones and so on. Or they can write them down on a piece of paper and put it in a safe place. And be sure to let someone know where that safe place is."

"What if you have no one to let your wishes be known to or to tell where the piece of paper is?" Garth asked.

"Then you attach it to your fridge with a fridge magnet," Emma said.

"That's a good idea, Em." Frank drained his mug. "Is there any more of that cocoa?"

"I'll make some more," Emma said. "I don't think anyone's very sleepy yet."

"Yeah, what the heck," Frank said.

The next morning when he was getting cream for his coffee Frank saw a piece of foolscap attached firmly to the fridge with a magnet on each corner. He recognized Garth's backhanded printing:

I Garth Foote wish to be kreemated when I die. Thanks.

And then his carefully written signature.

Frank would have preferred that his son's wishes involved going to the Red River Exhibition or maybe taking swimming lessons this summer, but what could you do? Garth had made his wishes known.

Frank began to think up some answers for questions he figured would be coming up in the near future. Avalanches, earthquakes and other natural disasters that could result in someone being buried alive. But not on the Canadian prairies.

CHAPTER 56
1975

Ivy has been employed for six years as a legal secretary at the firm of Grace, Royston & Wells on Portage Avenue. She has been promoted to the position of personal secretary to Simon Grace, a founder and partner in the firm. He pays her one hundred dollars a week to start. She has paid Wilf back the money he fronted her when she first left home.

Ivy has set up a life for herself in an apartment on Dorchester Avenue for which she pays one hundred and twenty dollars a month. She drives a '59 Chevy that she bought from the brother of one of the girls at work.

She has no real friends. That has never come easily to her. But the girls in the office seem to respect her position and her abilities. No one types faster than she does. They invite her to showers and for drinks after work. Sometimes she joins in, mostly she doesn't.

Simon Grace admires Ivy Srutwa; he finds her beautiful. It takes her a while to notice this and to really understand what it could mean for her. When he tries to kiss her, she lets him. She doesn't like it, but she doesn't hate it because she's concentrating on the larger good: Simon Grace can save her.

She tells him she's from Victoria. She admits to a brother, Wilf, but to no other ties. Her brother is ten years older than she is, but she doesn't tell Simon that he has a different dad. She doesn't want any suggestion of sleaziness sticking to her. Because of the age difference, she says, she never really got to know her brother. They see very little of each other.

Simon Grace never meets Wilf Srutwa.

In 1975, he marries Ivy.

She doesn't invite her brother to the wedding. She doesn't want to risk it.

CHAPTER 57
The Present

Simon wanted to please her. Ivy's pool was built in a hurry and it was almost as big as the one at the golf club. The workers had to chop down a poplar and three weeping birches to do it, but other than that, it was just a matter of digging up the lawn.

Simon hated to see the birches go, the quiet trees he'd had planted himself. He liked the way their leaves didn't fall in the winter. Once, during an ice storm, way back before Ivy, each leaf had looked as if it were encased in glass. The wind, a warm wind for January, blew through the leaves and they made a delicate clattering sound. Simon thought it was the most beautiful sound he had ever heard. He felt it in his gut, even now with the memory. He would never hear that sound again.

On a Saturday, just past mid-June, the pool was ready. Ivy swam and Simon watched. He had never seen her like this. He hadn't known there could be such a thing as a happy Ivy. She swam and then she wrote in that book of hers. Oh, how I would love to get my hands on that notebook, he thought.

There wasn't much in Ivy's notebook because she burned the pages after she was done with them. All the notes she had made relating to Task Number One had been destroyed.

It was Task Number Two she was thinking about now and the joy of it was she would be able to concentrate so much better now that she had her own pool.

Reuben had led her to this task. She waited for him to come now and he did. He was always there. It sometimes just took him a while to make his way to the front. With the voice came a taste, a flavour that was too faint to hold onto long enough to name. Sometimes it seemed more of a texture than a taste. Grit?

At first she had fought Reuben on Task Two because he seemed off base with what he said. Surely all these years later the mother was in the ground or scattered to the winds or in a can somewhere. But he persisted and anyway, Ivy knew it deep inside.

Sure enough, when she contacted Wilf, he confirmed that Olive's heart was still beating.

"I haven't seen her, though," Wilf said. "I haven't laid eyes on her since the day I dropped her off—what was it?—six years ago."

"But you know that she's still alive," Ivy said.

"Oh yeah, they'd have contacted me if anything had happened."

Wilf lived out east in Ontario, a place called Brockville. They hadn't spoken to each other since he tracked her down to tell her that he was placing Olive in a home because she could no longer manage on her own. She was soiling herself and lighting things on fire.

The manager of Olive's apartment block in Winnipeg had contacted Wilf and told him that it was time for her to go. Wilf arrived at his mother's suite, smelled her filth in the hallway and read the scrawled letters on the wall beside her door:

MRS. POO-PANTS LIVES HERE!

He found Ivy to tell her, figured she should know. She had told him then, six years ago, that it hadn't been necessary for him to get in touch, so she wasn't surprised not to have heard from him since.

Wilf was an important part of Ivy's past. He'd always been there in the background. It was his money that had supported Olive and her all the years she lived at home, ever since he had been old enough to hold a job. Always at the Bay. He had started in men's shoes and that's where he still was as far as Ivy knew. Just at a different Bay in a different city. At least he got away.

"Why do you ask?" Wilf said now. "Are you going to visit her?"

"Maybe."

"Why?"

"I don't know. She's my mother." Ivy was tempted to come clean, to tell Wilf what she intended to do, but she knew it wasn't safe to do that, not yet.

She had some nasty thoughts. What if I didn't get the HIV virus from that guy in Vancouver? The test could have been wrong. What if I'm not going to die? What if Wim Winston isn't going to die after all those hours of bloody sex?

She had bitten Wim's lip on that last night, hard enough to draw blood. And she had pulled out her own tooth! Ivy couldn't bear to think that all her hard work had been in vain. None of this would be any good if she wasn't going to die soon. She put the thought out of her head—she'd had the test. She carried the disease. But she decided to proceed with caution anyway. There was no need to broadcast her plans.

"So where is she?" Ivy asked.

"Just a minute and I'll get you the address and phone number."

Ivy turned to a new page in her notebook and copied Wilf's words. She ripped out the preceding page—the page that said: Phone Wilf.

The nursing home was in the Osborne Village area, which Ivy knew well. On many occasions she had passed by the building where her mother had lived for the past six years. She remembered noticing the residents outside on warm days, drooped in their chairs, breathing in exhaust fumes as the traffic whizzed past on Stradbrook Avenue. It was possible that one of those outdoor sitters had been her mother.

"Thanks, Wilf," she said. "Take care now."

"Wait, Ivy! God! Shouldn't we be asking each other how we are? How are you? How's Simon? How's life treating you?"

"Fine, thanks, Wilf. I really do have to go. Something's burning. Bye now."

Ivy watched the "Phone Wilf" page disintegrate into ashes in the ashtray, which she seldom used for cigarettes these days. She was losing her desire to smoke, but liked to have ashtrays in all the usual places for her regular burnings. This one was beside a comfy lawn chair next to her new swimming pool.

"Life feels good," Ivy said and closed her eyes against the sun. I'll just lie here awhile and then pop in for another swim.

CHAPTER 58

No matter how flat the afternoon or hollow the evening, no matter how dark the night, the summer mornings nudge Ivy to life, even if only for a few seconds while she remembers something sweet that never happened or a place she's never been. A soft fragrant breeze wafts against her face and she feels smooth and new and innocent. The moment of quiet is eternal and she sees her young self and Ray, riding their bikes no hands to the river. The slow-moving Red.

Ivy asked for directions to her mother's room. She wished the staff weren't so interested in her. She wanted just to slide in and slide out with barely a ripple, the way she does when she slips through the turquoise surface of her swimming pool.

But they fussed over her.

"Well, I declare!" an aide exclaimed. Her name tag said: Harriet Fimster.

"I didn't even realize that Olive had a daughter," she went on. "Have you traveled far, dear, to see your mum?"

"Yes, actually," Ivy said. "I've just flown in from Kuala Lumpur."

It still mattered to her that complete strangers not know the sour nature of the relationship between her and her mother.

"Goodness, that does sound far away," Harriet said.

"Yes, it is. That's where I live."

What harm are lies compared to the deed I have come for? I should have just said, friend of the family. It would have made me less noticeable.

Perhaps sour is too vital a word to describe what's between Olive and me, Ivy thought. It implies something that still has life in it. Well, there must be something in it, or I wouldn't be standing here now, telling lies to a harmless old nurse's aide. As long my mother draws breath, there's a connection between us.

"Could you point me in the right direction, please? I don't have a lot of time."

Harriet Fimster guided Ivy down a hall peopled with elderly residents: sitting, standing, staring, drooling, snoozing, sloping, dying. They all looked like her mother. Even the men looked like her mother. She wouldn't have been surprised had the aide stopped at any one of these people and announced that this was Olive Srutwa.

Olive was in a room with three others. Two of her roommates were missing. They must have been part of the hordes roaming the halls. Harriet left Ivy at the door, perhaps guessing that it was going to be a less than merry reunion. Ivy didn't want her to go. For one thing, she wasn't sure which of these creatures was related to her. She was going to have to get much closer and the one seated at the window looked insane.

"Yoo-hoo," the old crone cried out. "Over here, dear. I'm over here."

Ivy walked over to the window and peered into a wizened face. "Mum?"

"Yoo-hoo, over here, dear!" The woman blasted noise and foul air at Ivy, knocking her backwards toward the other bed, where her mother lay dying.

The figure on the bed barely made a rise in the blankets. It was so thin. Ivy stared at the familiar face. How could she have thought she wouldn't know her? Some of the lines and bumps were in the same places as Ivy's own lines and bumps had been before she'd had the cosmetic surgery done on her face and neck.

Her mother's eyes were closed and she breathed with difficulty.

A tender feeling flowed through Ivy and confusion clouded her brain, threatening to spoil her plan.

What Olive had done with the baby that she tore from her daughter's young body remained a mystery. It was only in Ivy's mind that she saw the tiny creature alone by the river's edge.

"He was alive," Ivy said and understood where her feelings of tenderness belonged. "My baby boy was alive. What did you do with him?"

Olive's eyelids snapped open. The whites of her eyes were a dull yellow—the wakened face a grotesque mask of death.

"Ivy, is that you?" Her voice scratched out the words. It was as if she hadn't spoken in years. Maybe she hadn't. Her eyes closed again.

"I did what had to be done."

Her breaths came more quickly now, like those of a smaller animal, one with a much shorter life span, like a squirrel.

The woman at the window fussed and mumbled. Ivy walked over to where she sat and turned the wheelchair so it faced away from Olive. She saw the name above the woman's bed. Annie Parrot.

"Okay, Annie baby. Let's just get you pointed in a different direction, shall we? A little different view for you. There we go. You can look at the pretty beige wall for a while."

"Yoo-hoo," Annie Parrot said softly.

From a bar fastened to Olive's bedside table hung a threadbare hand towel. Ivy reached for it. An odour rose from the towel, a dark, familiar stench, one that had haunted the edge of her memory all the days of her life. Her mother's fear; fear of her mother. A lifetime of fear scrunched up in a thin dank towel.

Ivy placed it over her mother's face and pressed firmly for twenty-nine seconds. That was all it took. The eyes didn't open again and there was the smallest struggle imaginable, a few twitches.

"Yoo-hoo!" called Annie Parrot as Ivy returned the hand-towel to the bar on the bedside table.

She poked her head out the door.

"Nurse Fimster," she called. "Could you come, please?"

Ivy sails down Osborne Street toward her car. The sky is so blue. It has never been so blue. Ivy feels as though she has completed the definitive act of her life. She smiles at the deadbeats and stops to pat their dogs. In Ivy's eyes, the street people glow. The air around her is so clean and pure she can see all the way to Riverview and all the way to Ray.

She pictures him on his bike at the top of the paths they call the Monkey Speedway. He rides the trails faster than anyone. He's the champ! He lets her accompany him, even though she's a girl with a girl's slow bike. And she's scared to go fast. They find the circle of stones in the clearing and he builds a smudgy fire with sticks and leaves and wooden matches from Winnipeg Supply. They heat a can of beans. And pull crabapples and plums from their pockets. Big kids come and they leave her alone because she's with her brother Ray, the champion of the Monkey Speedway.

Ivy stops for a cappuccino at Baked Expectations and wonders why she has never done this before. She sits outside and watches the world pass. The air is hers to breathe and the ground hers to walk on.

CHAPTER 59

Emma dreamed about Byron, her big old tabby cat who had died about a year ago. She often met him in her dreams. He was always glad to see her and would place his warm loving face next to hers. Tonight's dream started the same but turned out differently.

She sees her cat and moves toward him. He seems a little odd around the eyes. Her new cat Hugh is there too. She pats them both and grows uneasy when she notices that Byron feels cool to the touch. She pats warm Hugh and then cool Byron and the coolness passes through her fingers into her body.

The two cats scamper down some stairs and she is glad Byron is gone. He scares her. Emma knows she is dreaming now and worries that her good dreams of Byron will never be the same.

She peers down the stairs, willing the cat to stay away. He creeps into view and lunges toward her open face, screaming like a human.

Emma's own cry woke her up.

The house stood still around her. She hoped she hadn't woken anyone. She lay chilly under her quilt staring at the darkness in front of her eyes. Byron in her dreams had been something to look forward to, something she could count on as a good thing. This dream seemed like a cruel trick to her, something she didn't deserve. She was prepared for fear in the waking hours. But how could whoever was in charge of dreams have thought it was a good idea to turn Byron against her? It was so not right.

Emma believed in God, but only because she was scared not to. She found no comfort in a looming presence that operated against her. She prayed anyway. Maybe God did love her and had just made a mistake or lost track of things for a moment or two.

"You know what really bugs me, Dad?"

It was morning now and Emma was home from her papers. She had the *Free Press* opened to the obituaries.

"What?" Frank was trying to catch up on the Winnipeg Blue Bomber news which was on the front page of the section Emma was reading.

"I wish they wouldn't always put the deaths and the sports in the same section," he said. "I wonder if other families have this problem."

"What bugs me," said Emma, "is that about a thousand days ago it said: 'Longer obituary to follow,' after Esme Jones' death announcement, and then it never happened. Nothing followed."

"Maybe you just missed it," Frank said.

"I knew you'd say that. I didn't miss it. I checked every day."

"Well, maybe the people close to her felt so sad that they didn't feel up to writing a longer version."

"That's no excuse," Emma said. "She deserves better."

"Maybe it's still coming. Maybe her brother wanted to write it and he was in a car accident that resulted in a coma and they have to wait till he snaps out of it. They probably think he'd be upset if someone else went ahead and did it instead."

Emma laughed. "That's a little far-fetched isn't it?"

"Yup, but life is far-fetched, Emma, don't you think? How's the volcano coming?"

"Great! It's practically done. We just haven't rehearsed the actual eruption part. In case when we do, it wrecks the volcano. I'll save it for the presentation."

"When's that?"

"Wednesday. The day after tomorrow. I sure hope nothing goes wrong."

"I'm sure it won't, Em. You're certain to be the belle of science project day."

"Dad. You say the stupidest things sometimes. Here's the Sports Section. I gotta go. I'm meeting Donald before school. He's got some stuff called graphite he wants to show me."

"Oh yeah. Graphite. We have that stuff at the office. What does Donald plan to do with it?"

"He says it's black and kind of smoky lookin'. So we're thinkin' it could maybe add little puffs of smoke to the volcano if we can rig it up properly."

"Great idea!" Frank drained his coffee cup. He was so glad that he liked Donald. The idea of Emma and Donald busy with little bursts of greasy smoke made him positively jubilant.

CHAPTER 60

Frank dropped his car off at Minute Muffler on the way home from work on Tuesday and walked the rest of the way. On Lyndale Drive he passed four different sets of people and their dogs. Two of the dogs were Labradors and they were the two that made a point of coming over to see him. On the weekend he'd take Emma to the Humane Society to pick one out. Hopefully there'd be a Lab, or at least a mongrel with lots of Lab in it.

Frank looked forward to having a dog in the family, now that he was used to the idea. He had discussed it with Denise and she seemed fine with it. She liked dogs all right.

He had driven her to the group home today, and it had gone rather nicely, he thought, except for the part when she said it was good to die young. Oh, and the part where she didn't want to talk about Donald and how great he was. Other than that she had chatted with him and smiled at him and appeared bright in the shade of the old oaks.

"It's funny, isn't it, Frank," she had said, "the types of things that stay with you over the years? I remember the silliest things."

They were sitting at a picnic table in the yard of the old house on River Avenue where Denise was stationed for the next phase of her recovery, as they called it. This thing she was doing that Frank was afraid to hope for.

"And if I ever learned anything important," she went on, "I sure don't recall it now."

"What silly thing are you thinking about?" Frank asked.

Denise lit a cigarette and inhaled deeply, as if to force the nicotine along to every drug-starved nook and cranny in her body.

"Well, I had this aunt, Aunt Floss," she said. "Her name was Florence, but no one called her that. She was all pink and fluffy and she moved about in clouds of powder and perfume. Her job was being a cosmetics clerk at The Bay."

"I've never heard of Aunt Flossie before." Frank reached across for Denise's free hand.

"Just Floss." She laughed.

Frank knew that one day when Denise laughed like that it would be for the last time. And he might not be there for it. And even if he was, he wouldn't know it was the last time. This could be it, right now! This could be her last laugh.

"Anyway," Denise said, "she was my dad's oldest sister. She's dead now. Died pretty young of a heart attack; she was forty-four I think. A good age to die."

"Why on earth would you think forty-four is a good age to die?" Frank asked. "That's younger than me. It's awfully young, don't you think?"

"No." She stubbed out her cigarette in the ashtray where it joined an assortment of other butts.

The wind rose at that moment and all the ashes from the ashtray blew away, many of them into Denise's face. Frank wished they had landed on him instead. It seemed a very nasty thing to have happened to his wife. But she didn't seem to mind. He considered telling her about Garth's wish to be cremated and then decided it wasn't the right time. It was, after all, a rather dark anecdote.

"Floss gave me one of the most useless pieces of advice I've ever received from a person, but it's one that stuck with me."

"What was it?" Frank pushed the ashtray with its naked butts to the far end of the table.

"When she came to visit us," Denise said, "she used to sleep in my room with me and I would stand and watch while she went through her beauty routine."

"Did she sleep in your bed with you?" Frank asked.

"Yeah, she did."

"That must have been weird."

"I don't remember that part of it being weird." Denise lit another cigarette. "Are you going to let me tell my story?"

"Yeah. Sorry. Go ahead."

"Okay. So Floss would set herself up at my desk with her makeup mirror and a whole bunch of little pots of goop. She'd undress from the waist up and I would stare at her swaying breasts and the soft rolls of fat that folded over the waistband of her half slip.

"Her advice was: 'Always remember, Denise, that in the world of skin care, the face includes the neck, the chest and the breasts too.' She'd place her hand flat under her breasts till it disappeared entirely, to show me where her face ended and the rest of her began. I would be bundled in my flannelette pajamas, housecoat and slippers, watching Floss in her flimsy slip, her breasts pointed towards the floor, bravely rubbing the perfumed lotions into her skin. Anyway, I retained that particular piece of advice."

Frank was lost in the picture of Floss' downward pointing breasts.

He digested the story and watched Denise smoke. She flicked her butt onto the grass, where it smoldered and died. Frank forced himself not to retrieve it and place it in the ashtray where it belonged.

"Emma has a boyfriend," he said.

"Oh yeah?" Denise lit yet another cigarette.

"His name's Donald Griffiths and he seems really nice."

"Hmm."

"He helped Em build a volcano for her science project."

"Frank, let's not talk about Emma's boyfriend, okay? I don't feel strong enough to deal with it right now."

"Yes. All right. Sorry," Frank said. What the hell was there to deal with? This was good news, wasn't it? He wondered if Denise was jealous of Emma, of her starting out with her first boyfriend. It was possible. He'd heard of mothers being jealous of daughters. He'd just never thought of it happening in his own family. Well, he wasn't going to try to get to the bottom of it today and ruin the reasonably upbeat mood.

Yes, Frank thought now, as he watched the sun work its magic on the filthy waters of the Red, it had been a pretty good visit. She hadn't wanted to know about Donald and that was too bad, but she had talked up a storm otherwise.

Nothing hurt, Frank realized, as he walked briskly down the drive. Heel lifts in his shoes had solved his aching ankles problem—just like Gus had said they would.

He sang as he followed the river the rest of the way home, a song by a group called Fever Tree from a long time ago:

"Out there it's summertime, milk and honey days,
Oh, San Francisco girls with San Francisco ways."

Where did that come from? he wondered. He passed the Monkey Speedway, where in his youth he had performed daring feats on his bicycle. It was quiet. No boys rode there anymore.

CHAPTER 61

Emma set her volcano out on the front porch. It was Wednesday, Science Project Day, and she was late. Her papers had been slow to arrive at the drop-off spot and she hadn't been able to make up the time. Frank and Sadie came to the door to see her off.

"Be careful now, Em. You've got lots of time," Frank said. "It's okay if you're a few minutes late. You don't wanna trip and hurt yourself."

"Or your volcano," Sadie said.

"I should probably have covered it with something." Emma crouched in the front hall tying one runner, then the other. "I think it's gonna rain."

"Do you want an umbrella?" Sadie asked.

"No, silly. Then I would have only one hand to carry this thing that I need three hands to carry."

"Let's go with her, Sadie," Frank said. "We can help."

"Yay!" Sadie was still in her pajamas and bare feet but headed out the door and down the steps.

"Come back, you crazy nut," Frank said. "We're going to have to get you dressed first."

"I gotta go," Emma said. "Thanks, you guys, but I have no time."

"I can give you a ride home after school if you like. I should have the car back by then."

"It's okay, Dad. I'll be leaving the volcano at the school for a while. They're gonna make a display of the best projects and mine'll make it for sure."

By the time Emma was halfway to school the rain was pouring down in earnest. She stopped in a carport to examine the damage. The volcano was getting soggy but could still be saved if it didn't get any wetter. She would have to wait out the storm. I should have planned this better, she thought.

Donald had offered to come over and help her carry it, but she had turned down the offer. She didn't want to seem needy. Now she realized how stupid that was. He had helped her every other step of the way.

Oh God, why didn't I let him? Tears of frustration streamed down her face as she stared out from under the leaky carport connected to the garage of someone she didn't know.

The top of the volcano collapsed in on itself and she set it down on the cement and busied herself with fixing it. A piece came off in her hand and then another.

A car drove up and a window rolled down.

"Can I offer you a lift, dear?"

Emma looked up to see a pretty woman with her hair pulled back in a pony tail. She was dry as chalk. Emma couldn't recall ever having seen her before, with her jaunty head band and sporty car.

"Here, let me help you." The woman got out of the car and crouched down in her pink track suit next to Emma who held squashed pieces of papier mâché in her hands.

The woman smelled like cookies. "Oh dear. Let's get this into the trunk and I'll give you a ride to school. Is that where you're headed?"

Emma nodded and watched her volcano being placed in the trunk next to the woman's gym bag. She walked around to the passenger side of the car and got in. As soon as she had done this she knew she had made a mistake. Even before the smiling woman flipped the locks on the doors and windows into place.

The rain stopped as suddenly as it started and the sun came out.

"That makes things better doesn't it, Emma, to see the sun, I mean?"

"How did you know my name?"

The tiny hairs on the back of Emma's neck stood up. She watched the woman light a Matinee and wheel the car north in the opposite direction from the school.

"Where're you going?" Emma's voice was reedy and thin. "This isn't the way."

"I just want to show you something, dear. You're already late. A little while longer won't matter."

Emma tried the door when they came to a stop sign. It wouldn't open. She tried the window. It wouldn't open either.

"Please let me out." She couldn't hear her own words and didn't know if she had spoken them aloud. So she tried again. Same thing.

Ivy parked as close to the penalty box as she could get. When she opened her door, Emma scrambled to get by her, but Ivy placed her hand on the girl's face and pushed her so hard that her head hit the window on the passenger side.

Ivy opened the trunk and took the handcuffs and duct tape out of her gym bag, then got back into the car with the girl, who had started to scream. It was easy to get the cuffs on. Ivy's arms were strong. She knew how important strength was to her task. Tape the mouth. There. Quiet was much better.

Ivy locked the girl in the car while she carried her supplies to the penalty box. Then she dragged the struggling girl there too. She set to work, first removing the runners, jeans and underwear. Everything was so small. From her bag she took the heavy twine and Swiss army knife. She tied the ankles to two posts that were almost too far apart. It was as though this penalty box had been custom made for the two of them. There was a sound then, one that Ivy had heard before, something to do with Sunday dinner— chicken legs.

Emma saw the woman as though from a distance. Like when she looked through the wrong end of her dad's binoculars at Blue Bomber games and the players and the crowd got small. She saw her ankles secured to posts at an impossible distance from her body.

The hurt in her legs, at their tops where they joined her hips was almost familiar to her but not from actual experience. It was how she had imagined pain when she pictured worse stuff happening to her than anything that possibly could. Pain like what she saw on the Discovery Channel, when the lions tore apart the antelopes and the foxes devoured the mice.

She had a bit of trouble recognizing it at first. It was separate from her and she tried to keep it aside, something to deal with later, when she felt up to it and could make sense of it. It only interfered now with the main event. Or maybe it was the main event. She didn't know.

Is there something I could be doing to make this right? she wondered. Or is it too late? She groaned and the woman pinched her nose so that she couldn't breathe at all.

"Be quiet please, Frank's girl," the woman said and let go of her nose. She was so far away through the backward binoculars that Emma was amazed she was able to connect with her at all. She shivered inside her sodden T-shirt and prayed for anything to happen that would save her.

Gus whistled his way through the rain-drenched streets in his old Buick with the windows rolled down. The sun shone and the morning sparkled. He was going to check on some new cement. The sidewalk between the two hockey rinks had been poured yesterday afternoon and Gus had sowed a layer of seed minutes after the workmen had finished. He hoped the birds had found it. It was a little out of the way, with few trees about, but the birds hadn't let him down yet and he didn't expect they would today.

He parked where the old pleasure rink used to be, beside a little red Triumph that he eyed suspiciously. He hadn't expected to run into anyone this early on a school day. The last thing he wanted was an audience. Gus cursed his knees as he struggled out of the driver's seat. He heard the low talking first and didn't know where it was coming from. The sports car was the only sign that there was anyone else around. It was a female voice he heard and he didn't like the sound of it. Gus stood still. The voice was quiet now, but he heard a soft clanking sound coming from one of the penalty boxes. Metal rattling against metal. Cold and hard.

Then he saw a woman's head with black hair pulled back in a pony tail. She hadn't seen him, so intent was she on something beneath her in the box. Gus' first thought was that it was a young couple making out. Having no place to go was nothing new.

But the woman didn't look like she was loving anybody and it was then that Gus recognized her as the no-gooder from the graveyard. The one with the car the same colour as Lake Winnipeg. She had a different car today.

He never had mentioned her to Frank. He should have.

Alarm rang in his ears as he limped toward the penalty box. His legs wouldn't move fast enough. He began to shout before he got there to stop whatever this horrible woman was up to.

"Ray?" she asked, looking through Gus.

"Good God in heaven, what's going on here?" Gus pushed Ivy aside and fell to his knees at Emma's feet, untying her small ankles first to begin to undo the worst of it.

"Oh Ray, you've come to help us. I knew you would. Why did you go? Why didn't you come sooner?"

Ivy bent to take Emma in her arms and Gus screamed at her to get away.

"Give me the key!" he hissed.

"What key?"

"The key for the handcuffs, you crazed hunk of insanity!"

"Squirk," Ivy whispered.

Gus gently placed his cardigan over Emma's bottom half. Her body didn't look right and her eyes were closed. But she was breathing and her pulse was strong.

When he stood up he saw the dog named Easy in the baseball field past the community club. And the man Rupe, throwing a stick for the dog.

"Help!" Gus shouted at the top of his lungs. "Help please, Rupe, Easy!"

Ivy covered her ears and slid to a crouch in a corner of the penalty box.

Gus had been worried that she would make a break for it, but the creature cowering on the ground didn't look as though she would be running anywhere anytime soon. She faced the wall and he could hear squeaky sounds coming from her throat. Mouse sounds. This person was insane.

And who the hell was Ray?

Easy and Rupe appeared at the gate to the penalty box.

"Holy hell," Rupe said.

"Run somewhere and phone an ambulance, will ya?" Gus said. "I can't leave either of these people."

Rupe was already dialing the phone that he carried in his pocket and Gus added a fourth thing to the list of inventions he appreciated that had come after the second world war.

CHAPTER 62

Frank sat at the kitchen table reading the obituaries. The face that stared back at him was older than its previous incarnation, the one of the happy child in a baseball cap that Emma had pointed out to him a few weeks ago. On this face the eyelids drooped as if to protect the eyes from a vision seen once that they couldn't bear to witness again in its entirety. The mouth was pinched shut. The smiling girl had been replaced.

Esme Jones, the long version:

Esme died suddenly, at home on May 3, 1995 at the age of fourteen.

She is survived by her father Edward; brother Ross; sister Jennifer; grandparents; aunts; uncles; and cousins. She was predeceased by her mother, Louise Jones, in 1991.

Esme's hobbies were looking after her pets: Louie (dog), Mickey (cat), and Tweetie (bird); and geology. She was very interested in rock formations.

Esme will be long remembered for her sense of humour, her kindness, and her gentle ways.

Thanks to Dr. Jill Lazarenko for her valiant efforts in fighting for our Esme's health.

A private service has been held and interment has taken place in Brookside Cemetery.

Donations may be made in Esme's name to the Schizophrenia Society Inc. Manitoba.

We'll never forget you, our sad, brave girl.

Frank would take it to Emma in the hospital. It wasn't much of an offering but he knew she would want to see it.

"She's perfect, Dad," Emma said from her hospital bed when Frank snuck the new Labrador pup in to see her.

"She is, isn't she, Em?" Frank kissed his daughter on the forehead. "She already has a name, I'm afraid: Doris. But I'm sure she's young enough that she wouldn't mind if you wanted to change it." He placed the pup in Emma's arms.

"Oh, Dad. Look at her."

"Look at you." Frank pulled his chair up as close as he could to Emma's bed.

"Doris is fine as a name," Emma said. "I kinda like it."

The little dog licked Emma's face and squirmed about excitedly for a bit and then settled in for a snooze in her arms. Frank had played vigorously with the puppy before bringing her to the hospital, in order to tire her out.

Emma had suffered a dislocated hip during her ordeal. That part of it was something that could be made right again. The rest of it, Frank was less sure about.

He ached at the sight of her slight frame cuddling the puppy. Emma was stronger than she looked. But how could a thirteen-year-old come out unscathed on the other side of a trip to hell? She couldn't. It was the stuff of lives that turned out like Ivy Srutwa-Grace's life.

But Ivy'd had no one to love her. And Emma did. She did and always had.

He thought about the easy way that she'd said "I hate her" when talking about Denise. And he thought about Denise's lack of interest in Donald Griffiths, her daughter's first boyfriend. Emma hadn't seen her mother for a month and a half.

Frank pushed the hair back from her eyes. "Oh, Em."

"Do you know what became of my volcano?" she asked.

"Yes. Gus took it home. Donald's coming to get it today. He asked that same question."

"Does he know what happened to me?"

Frank had spoken to Donald himself when the boy phoned to find out why Emma hadn't turned up on Science Project Day.

"I should've come over to help her carry it to school," Donald said. "I should've insisted."

"It's not your fault, Donald. Not even a little bit."

"Is she okay? Is she gonna be okay?"

"She's hurt," Frank had said. "But yeah, she's going to be okay."

Frank covered one of his daughter's hands with his own. "Donald doesn't know the details. He wants to know if he can come to see you. Delia too."

"Why did this happen to me, Dad?" Emma asked. "Who is she? She called me Frank's girl."

She knows it has everything to do with me, Frank thought.

"I'm going to tell you, Emma, as best I can, but not right now. Let's wait till you're physically a little better so you don't have too much to think about all at once. Dr. Kowalski says you're doing great, by the way."

"Tell me now, Dad."

"What about Doris?"

"Doris is asleep." She kissed the puppy's head.

She won't love me anymore after I tell her, Frank knew. I'm about to grind salt into the gaping wound of the person I love best in the world.

"I love you, Emma," he said. "No matter how much you don't love me, nothing's going to change that, ever."

"Why would I not love you?" Fear filled her eyes. "How could I not love you?"

Frank told her about his part in the rape of Ivy Srutwa. The parts about how he didn't actually do it, and how he argued with the other boys and finally how he was the one to untie her, those parts rang hollow. They sounded like words that someone else should be saying in his defense, Ivy maybe. From him they sounded pitiful. He felt like he was defending a boy who ripped wings off butterflies and set kittens on fire.

"You tied her?"

"Someone tied her. Yes."

"Like she did to me."

"Yes. Like she did to you."

Emma closed her eyes and was quiet for so long that Frank thought she had gone to sleep. He stood up and walked to the window.

"So you didn't actually do anything to her, then?" Emma said.

"No. No, I didn't. But I didn't stop it."

Frank stared out the window at the Red. Last summer he and Emma had canoed down the river from the Rowing Club to the Bridge Drive-In. They had gone ashore for milkshakes and then rowed all the way back.

"Where's Mum?" Emma asked.

"She's in a sort of residential home for recovering alcoholics," Frank said. "They're going to let her out this afternoon to come and visit you."

"I'd really like to see her." Emma started to cry. "I miss her."

Frank reached out but she stiffened at his touch.

"I'm kinda tired now, Dad. I think I'll sleep for a while." She spoke through her tears as she handed the little golden dog back to her father.

"Emma."

"Please go now, Dad."

Frank sat on a chair outside Emma's room until Doris woke up. Before he left, he looked in on his daughter who lay on her back staring at the ceiling, dry-eyed. She didn't look at him and he didn't bother her again that day.

He hadn't given her the obituary. Esme Jones had almost certainly killed herself. Maybe her mother had too. It wasn't a good gift for Emma now. He'd give it to her later. She had far too much to deal with right now. He knew he wouldn't hide it from her for long, though, because Emma would catch him out.

CHAPTER 63

Frank sat at his desk thinking about Ivy Grace. Over the last week he had found out a few things about Ivy, not the least being that she had probably killed her own mother.

He stared down at a report that Ed Flagston had dropped on his desk last Friday morning, two days after Emma's ordeal. The report contained the findings of the DNA test on Ivy's cigarette butt, and a comparison of those findings with the DNA of little Jane Doe. The lab was hanging on to her hair for further testing, but the cigarette butt was enough.

Frank's chest ached with thoughts of his daughter. He had been so relieved when she'd asked about Denise. She missed her mother. She didn't hate her anymore. Just him. Things would never be the same between them; he was a bad guy in Emma's eyes. He couldn't bear it. Yes, he could.

Ivy Grace must have hated her mother, Frank thought, as he closed his middle drawer on Emma's finished scarf. But Ivy was insane. Something had snapped in her. Who knew how these things happened? Her dad had hung himself in the basement of the family home. Ivy was probably marked long before the thugs got hold of her in the penalty box.

Frank couldn't bring himself to give Emma the scarf just yet. It seemed too lame a present after all that had happened.

He picked up his keys and headed out to his car.

Greta was sitting on her front steps waiting for him. She had two little pink boxes, both containing butter tarts—one box for Frank and one for Jane.

They made the short trip out of town to the River City Health Centre so that Greta could meet her daughter for the first time. Or the second, if you counted holding her for a few moments in 1968.

They were quiet on the drive out, each lost in thought. Frank reached into his little box and took out a tart. Then he put it back.

"What if she doesn't want to see me?" Greta said as they pulled into the parking lot.

"Then we'll turn around and drive home," Frank said. "But I don't think that's going to happen." He wasn't as sure as he sounded.

But it wasn't Jane he was thinking about.

Frank knew that Ivy Grace was somewhere in the vicinity, under lock and key for a period of evaluation. He worried that she wouldn't be guarded closely enough. She could escape and hurt someone. Emma.

He wondered if Ivy was looking out at him now as they walked down the white-hot sidewalk toward the shady stone steps of the administration building. His hands were cold and his feet were numb. He walked without moving his arms, his fists clenched tightly at his sides. All natural motion left him as he lurched toward their destination.

Inside the door he found a water fountain where he drank and drank till he realized that his thirst would not be satisfied. He straightened up and accompanied Greta to take care of the business at hand, which had nothing to do with Ivy.

Frank walked with her as far as the door to Jane's room. Then he stepped back and let her go in alone. He found a chair where he sat awhile but he couldn't get comfortable. So he stood up and paced the sunny institutional halls.

He pictured Ivy Grace, the smooth face that she had paid to have pulled and stretched to wipe out any living that she had done. Crazy as a shithouse rat.

Greta stayed with Jane for a long time. Frank was glad of this; it was a good thing.

She was quiet on the way home, but there was a peacefulness about her. Frank didn't ask any questions.

"Thanks, Frank," she said when she got out of the car. "Thanks for everything."

"It's okay, Greta."

"Maybe sometime you'd like to visit Jane with me. We could take her out somewhere."

"That'd be nice," Frank said, but all he could think about was Emma.

He turned his smoothly running Toyota into the parking lot of the Bridge Drive-In where he sat in his car and stared at the river awhile before strolling up to the counter.

"A chocolate milkshake please, thin."

"Here, let me get that," said a voice behind him and he turned to see Gus.

They hadn't seen much of each other the past few days. After the horror of last Wednesday they had both needed a little time. They hadn't been avoiding each other really, just not seeking one another out.

"I need to talk to you, Frank," Gus said, and they started a slow walk over the Elm Park Bridge, milkshakes in hand.

"What is it, Gus?" Frank didn't feel up to much; he hoped it wasn't big.

"It's my fault, what happened to Emma." Gus stopped walking and rested his shake on a railing.

A dizziness washed over Frank and he sat down on a curb that had been built to separate the cyclists from the pedestrians. They didn't have the sense to stick to their own sides without it. The curb didn't seem to help much, but it gave Frank a place to sit.

"What on earth are you talking about, Gus? What do you mean it's your fault? Of course it isn't your fault." He set his milkshake aside and held onto his temples with both hands.

"Yeah, it is," Gus said and sat down beside Frank. "I'd seen that woman before. I meant to tell you about it, to discuss her with you, because she made me so nervous, but I never got around to it. Never in my wildest dreams did I imagine that she was actually dangerous. She scared me, but I thought it was just me being old. If I'd only told you about her, you could probably have nipped her in the bud."

"Whoa there, Gus. I'd seen her before too. Lots of times. I'd talked to her, Christ, I'd had lunch with her! Nothing's your fault. Do you hear me? You saved Emma, you and your odd little bird-seed hobby."

"You know about that?" Gus asked.

Frank smiled and put his arm around his friend. "Where did you see her, Gus?"

"On the street. Out front. She was driving slow and she stopped to ask me if that was where you lived. I didn't tell her. Like I said, she scared me. And she pointed to Greta's house and asked if that was where the Simkins lived. I didn't tell her that either."

Frank stared at Gus, who had turned his attention back to his milkshake. He had a right to know everything. And Frank would have to be the one to tell him. He did so now.

Afterwards they sat quietly on the curb and Gus finished his shake. Frank didn't even get started on his.

Finally, Gus spoke. "So the woman's saliva, this Ivy person's DNA, turned out to be the same as that poor little baby's."

"Yeah. The results came back last week, two days after Emma…"

"Oh, Frank." It was Gus' turn to put his arm around his friend. "Emma will be fine. You'll see."

"She'll get tested too, for the HIV virus, just to be on the safe side. But there wasn't any blood or anything. Thank God. There wasn't, was there, Gus?"

Last Wednesday was such a mess in Frank's head that he couldn't stay sure of anything. He knew that he knew this, but he had to check it again with Gus, hear him say it.

"No, Frank. There for sure wasn't. No worries there."

"Gus, thanks for the milkshake. Don't you worry about anything. Nothing's your fault. I mean it. Nothing." Frank was on his feet and walking quickly back across the bridge toward his car.

When asked, Ivy had freely admitted giving birth to a tiny baby last October, shortly after returning from Vancouver. She admitted to everything. Frank kicked himself for not just coming out and asking her in the first place. She probably would have told him. He'd been so busy tiptoeing around her. How could he not have realized what she was capable of?

She had punished the Simkin boys in her own mind by smothering her sick baby, wrapping it in swaddling clothes and laying it, no, dropping it into their rain barrel. A grisly offering, which never even reached the intended recipients, just their poor stepsister, Greta Bower. It was a crazy, horrendous, pitiful crime.

When Frank got back to the office there was a message on his machine from Wim Winston. It was urgent, said Wim. Something to do with a picture he had seen in the Free Press of this woman, Ivy Grace, who had been causing all kinds of trouble.

Frank didn't return Wim's call.

Frank took his family, minus Denise, plus Doris, to the lake. Gus and Donald came too. They all fit in the station wagon. Gus was more excited than any of them.

"I wonder if pelicans still turn up out there," he said.

"I'm sure they do, Gus. Why wouldn't they?" Frank asked.

"I don't know. I'm always hearing stories about whole species disappearing all of a sudden or turning into something else. Did you read that mutated frog story in the paper?"

"Yeah, actually, I did," Frank said. "That's not exactly turning into something else. I mean, they're still frogs. They just have an extra leg or two."

"Ew! Gross!" Garth said. "They probably wish they were dead."

"Frogs don't wish," said Emma. She was stretched out on a slab of foam in the back.

"How do you know?"

"I just do."

"I saw a pelican as recently as last summer," Donald said.

"Did you, Donald?" said Sadie. She had taken quite a shine to Emma's new friend and figured on marrying him some day.

"Yeah, how'd you know?" Donald asked.

Sadie whooped with laughter. "Oh, Donald!"

Frank followed Main Street to get out of town. It was either that or McPhillips and McPhillips made him feel glum. He didn't mention this. That a city street could affect him in this way wasn't something he felt he could share with his kids. Gus maybe. Regent Avenue did it to him too and St. James Street. Frank felt a little woozy just thinking about them.

Donald carried Emma and laid her gently on a blanket on the beach. He settled a legless beach chair behind her, an umbrella above her, and himself beside her. It was her fourteenth birthday.

Gus, Sadie and Doris frolicked at the water's edge.

Garth buried his head in a comic book. An Edgar Allan Poe comic book. What next? Frank wondered.

He watched the waves breaking on the shore. He walked to the edge of the water where it passed over small smooth stones. Past the stones was the sand where he had walked out and farther out on long ago boyhood days. Maybe if I keep on walking, Frank thought, if the sandbars take me further than I was ever able to go, maybe I can get to a place that went before. And change things some.

When he was up to his neck in Lake Winnipeg, he looked back to shore and saw his family. They were very small on the beach, but he could make each one out. Garth, fully clothed, with his comic book, Sadie at the shore line with Gus and Doris. There was one lone pelican south of his family in shallow water and Frank watched Gus gesturing wildly as he pointed it out to everyone. He tried to imagine what it would be like to get that excited about seeing a big white water bird. He couldn't.

Emma sat on her blanket beside Donald. Emma. Her hand was above her head. It took Frank a moment to realize what was happening. His daughter was waving at him. Who am I to warrant such a gift? he wondered. Who can I be that she sees fit to raise her hand to me? He waved back and his tears mixed with the lake as he made his way slowly back to shore.

ABOUT THE AUTHOR

Alison Preston was born and raised in Winnipeg. After trying on a number of other Canadian cities, she returned to Winnipeg, where she lives with her partner Bruce and their cat in Frank Foote's neighbourhood. A graduate of the University of Winnipeg, and a letter carrier for the past twenty years, Alison was nominated for the John Hirsch Award for Most Promising Manitoba Writer in 1998. Her first book, *A Blue and Golden Year*, was also a literary mystery.

AGMV Marquis

MEMBRE DU GROUPE SCABRINI

Québec, Canada
2000